THE HARD TRUTH

JESSICA RANEY

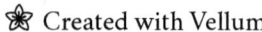

CHAPTER 1

"No freaking way am I taking that table, Tammi." Davida Barker shook her head as she shoved pink artificial sweetener packets into the sugar caddies. Her tables were clean and stocked. She was ready to cash out.

"Come on Davi," Tammi pleaded. "I gotta meet Steve downtown. It's his birthday."

"Tough shit. I have to pick up the kid from my mom's. She's already texted me ten times. Get Rick to take it."

"Rick already bounced. Please Davi? I'll give you ten to take it."

Davi looked over at the table. It wasn't her section, and it wasn't even her turn in the rotation, but she had a terrible feeling she was going to have to wait on the table anyway. It was five til eleven. The kitchen was breaking down, however the rules said they were open until eleven so even at five til, if people walked in, they had to be served. Cyndi, the idiot hostess, should have flipped the CLOSED sign early, but she was too slow; the couple walked in and asked for a booth before anybody could pretend the restaurant was closed.

Davi had drawn a closing shift, which was great because she needed the cash but bad because her mom's patience where babysitting was concerned was limited. Her mom had to be at work at six in the morning, and when Davi closed, she couldn't pick the kid up until at least midnight. She'd been lucky tonight and had done her closing work quickly. Then the table went down, and Tammi decided she was more interested in banging her boyfriend Steve down at the nasty sports bar than in working the last table.

Davi didn't like Tammi. She stole money and took tables that weren't hers, so it was ironic that she was trying to pawn one off on Davi. After a glance at the couple seated at booth twenty-three, Davi knew why. The guy was skinny and greasy with a patchy beard, a sparse mustache, and long hair tucked under a dirty backward baseball cap. He wore a ratty Pantera t-shirt and dirty jeans that looked like they could stand of their own accord. His companion was an anorexic-looking woman of indeterminate age who sported a distinctive look that Davi had named Oxy-Whore. She was painfully skinny, her arm bones and sternum clearly visible under sallow, stretched skin. Her dirty blonde hair was thin and pulled back in a tight pony tail that accentuated her frailty. Her dark-rimmed, glassy eyes didn't seem to be focused on anything and she swayed back and forth in the booth, barely able to stay upright.

"Shit," Davi sighed. "Twenty bucks, plus you do all my closing work tomorrow."

"Done. I'll give you the twenty tomorrow."

"Fuck you, Tammi. Give me it now or I bail." Davi held out her hand. She knew better than to trust Tammi to be good for anything other than blowing Steve in the shitter at the bar.

Tammi scowled and rummaged around in her apron. She pulled out a wad of cash and peeled off a twenty-dollar bill, then threw it down on the table. "You're kind of a cunt, Davi."

"Yeah, well, I'm not a dumb cunt," Davi smiled as she picked up the money and pocketed it. She grabbed some napkins and headed over to the booth.

It was worse than she thought. They smelled like cat piss, and when the man grinned, she saw he was missing several teeth. Davi read once in an anthropology book that loss of dentition in primates was a sign of higher evolution. That text book writer had never been to Denton County, where meth and oxytocin addictions accounted for major losses of dentition and significant de-evolution of the species.

"Evening. My name's Davi and I'll be taking care of you. Can I get you folks something to drink?" She slapped the beverage napkins down in front of them.

"Big Bud, one of them tall ones," the man said. He stared at Davi's tits.

She nodded at him then looked to the woman. "And for you, ma'am?"

"Just water for her," the man said as he continued to stare at Davi's chest and grin.

"Sure," Davi said. She headed to the bar to pour his beer. When she got back to the table she set the drinks down in front of them, and the man immediately chugged the tall draft beer. He drained it three-quarters of the way before he came up for air, belched, and wiped his lip with his sleeve.

"Whew. I was thirsty," he yelled, then laughed a wheezing, high-pitched laugh.

It made Davi's skin crawl and she barely stopped herself from wincing. "Yep," Davi nodded. "Looks like it. You folks decide on what you want to eat?"

"I want a steak. Well done. Give me double fries. Don't want no faggy salad or shit."

Davi didn't bother to write it down. She would have known how to cook it even if he hadn't told her.

"Sure thing. What can I get for you, ma'am?" Davi turned to the woman.

The woman looked over the menu. She turned the sticky pages slowly and seemed confused by the pictures. She raised her head and looked in Davi's general direction, but her eyes didn't focus on anything. "Chicken fingers," she managed to croak out.

"Yes ma'am," Davi nodded.

"Just the small ones," the man said as he finished his beer.

"Bring lots of ranch and ketchup." He lifted the empty beer glass and shook it in Davi's face. "More of these, too."

Davi took the glass. "Yes sir."

She chucked the empty glass into the bar sink and rang in the food order. Davi grinned when the cussing started in the kitchen and knew they had seen it come through. She deposited another beer for the man, then headed into the kitchen.

"What the fuck is this shit, Davi? I already closed the grill." Dustin, the douchey grill guy slammed things around in protest.

"What the hell does it look like? It's an order," Davi said.

"Tell 'em we're closed." Dustin threw his tongs down on his station.

"We ain't closed until eleven, and it wasn't eleven when dipshit sat 'em," Davi said. "So, get busy burning the shit out of his steak."

"This is fucked up. I was already closed."

"Yeah, well, I ain't thrilled about it either." Davi went behind the counter and dropped the fries and chicken fingers in the fryer herself. Billy, the fry side guy, was nowhere to be seen, and she knew he was most likely smoking weed with the kitchen manager out by the dumpster. She ignored Dustin's bitching and finished the food. When she delivered it to the table, the man had drained the second beer and the woman had fallen asleep.

"Fuckin' about time. What'd you have to do, kill the cow?" He wagged the beer glass in the air, slammed it down for emphasis, then dug into his over-cooked meat, which was a steaming slab of tough grey matter. "Ketchup," he said with his mouth full.

Davi reached over and grabbed it from the table. She set it in front of him. The woman didn't wake up for her chicken tenders and ranch dressing. "Would you like another beer or something else to drink?"

"Another Bud and a shot of Jack," he said around a mouthful of fries and meat. "What kind of name is Davi?" he asked when she came back with his drinks.

"It's short for Davida."

He laughed out loud after he downed the shot. "Davida's a fat girl's name." He took a long drink of the beer as he leered at her. "You ain't fat."

"Well, thanks, I guess," Davi said, not knowing exactly what to say that didn't involve the words fuck and off. "You guys want anything else?" She didn't give them much chance to answer as she put the check face-down on the table. "Ok, well, I'll be your cashier whenever you're ready. No rush." She walked off and down the two stairs that led into the bar area to finish cleaning.

Davi finished cleaning all the tables and when she turned around to check on the couple, she found herself face-to face with the man. The woman stood by the door, weaving back and forth. The man grinned at Davi, and he had something behind his back. "Umm, ready to pay—" Davi stopped talking when he shoved the handgun into her chest.

"I want your cash. All of it," he said.

Davi's heart thundered in her chest, and she felt prickly all over. Her hands shook as she untied her apron and held it up. He took it. "You the only one here?"

"Yep. Only one with cash, so just go on and let us be," she said.

"What about that register?" he asked as he nodded to the bar.

"Nope. Manager already took the drawer," Davi said.

"Well, guess there ain't nothing else to do here," he said. He smiled at her. She thought his face looked like a rat then. All thin and beady.

The noise didn't seem like a gunshot to her. All she heard was a loud whoosh, then she was flat on her back in the bar area and she couldn't breathe. Her chest was heavy and burning, and she could smell a funny smell—gunpowder and burnt hair—as she lay there. Davi felt like something was stuck in her throat, and she struggled to clear it. When she did, she spit out a big bubble of blood. She tried to move her arms, but they wouldn't move; they felt incredibly heavy to her, like they were suddenly made of lead. It registered then that he had shot her in the chest, and she began to panic. Her mind raced, but she couldn't move. Davi thought about her kid, sleeping on her mom's old sofa, waiting for her to pick him up and how she was going to be late. She thought she would black out, but she never did. Instead, the prickly feeling got stronger, then it radiated throughout her body. She was still and didn't know if she was breathing. She couldn't hear anything, but she could still see. Then her body started to tingle, like the whole thing had been a giant sleeping limb, and the sounds all rushed back to her ears. She sucked in a huge lung-full of air, then she sat up and screamed.

Davi looked down at her chest and saw a big burnt hole in her shirt. Her skin was raw and angry-red looking, but it was whole and intact. She ran her hands over it. Everything was still there, just tender and bloody—her sternum, her guts, her tits. She got to her feet. It took her a minute. She shook and weaved as she tried to regain her balance. When she stood fully upright, the man was still standing there with the gun, staring at her, his toothless mouth gaping. He clutched her apron and the gun. He dropped the gun but not her money, then ran from the restaurant.

Davi didn't follow. Instead, she stood there staring at the gun as her mind wrapped itself around the fact that she'd just been shot point-blank in the chest and somehow, she was still breathing.

CHAPTER 2

DAVI SIPPED a steaming hot cup of coffee. She pulled the blanket tighter around her body and waited impatiently for the cops to let her leave. They buzzed about, taking statements and gathering evidence.

She watched Gabe, the kitchen manager, his hands shaking as he handed the security recorder to the Sheriff. Gabe was high as a kite. His bloodshot eyes were all wild whites, and he twitched. The Law didn't care about a pothead restaurant manager—the sheriff was more interested in the thief—but you would never have convinced Gabe of it. He dropped the recorder twice when the big burly Sheriff waved him off and picked the thing up himself before it was destroyed.

Nobody was paying much attention to Davi. She had changed her shirt quick while they called the cops, then when they got there, she told them the guy only fired the gun at her but didn't hit anything. She knew nobody believed that, but she was quite sure they wouldn't believe she healed from a point-blank gunshot wound in about sixty seconds.

The sheriff was a big guy—barrel chested, bear-like—and he had kind eyes. Jacob was his name. She thought he seemed kind of young to be sheriff, but she guessed the shit stain county made do with what it had. If all it had was a young guy wanting to be sheriff, she figured that was what it was. He finished with Gabe and walked over to her. For such a big guy, he moved easy and sure, like a big cat.

"Miss Barker, you sure you're ok?"

Davi cleared her throat and nodded. She had called her mom and told her what happened. Her mom had sounded equal parts concerned and annoyed, which was normal. All Davi wanted was to get the hell out of there, grab the kid, and go home. "Yes sir, I'm alright. Can I go home now?"

He looked her over carefully. "And you're sure you told us everything?"

"I told you everything, Sheriff. I don't know what else you need to know."

"Well, it ain't every day you get shot at and robbed. Maybe you ain't exactly recalling everything. Maybe you're a bit shook up is all." He pulled a card out of his front shirt pocket and handed it to her. "You think of anything else, call me."

She took the card and looked it over, then nodded and stood up. She left the blanket. "Sure."

The Sheriff nodded at her shirt. "You always stay that clean of a shift?"

The uniform looked new and spotless. No crusty ranch dressing stains, no grease spots marred its front. It even had the fold crease still down the middle. Davi looked down at it and shrugged. "No, and I didn't tonight either. Spilled some shit on it and I changed."

"They charge you for that?" He motioned to her new shirt.

"They can try," Davi said, "But they won't know if I don't tell 'em. Considering tonight, I really don't care."

"Fair enough," the sheriff said. "Rough night for sure. You want me to give you a lift home?"

"No thanks. I got a car." Davi grabbed her bag and headed to the door.

"Miss Barker?"

She turned and looked at him, one hand on the front door handle. "Yeah?"

"You be careful." He tipped his hat to her, but he didn't smile.

Davi nodded then booked it out to her car. The beat-up Ford Focus had over a hundred thousand miles on it, and every time Davi put the key in the ignition, she wasn't entirely sure it was going to start. She shoved the key in and turned it. The engine whined and sputtered, but eventually came to life, coughing and wheezing like an old man. "Yeah, thanks, buddy. I ain't really got it in me to deal with you tonight." She often talked to the car. She'd had it for ten years, and it had become a kind of life partner to her. Shitty and old though he might have been, he stuck around. That was better than she could say for most of the other men in her life.

She pushed him as fast as she dared on the drive across town to her mom's place. When she got there, her mom was waiting up watching some infomercial on the Hallmark channel.

"Look Davida, I know you had you a night, and I'm glad you're ok, but we can't keep doing this." She stubbed out a cigarette and stood up.

Davi ignored her and went to the couch. Alex was asleep, balled up like usual. He was tiny for his age, and when he curled up like that, he looked even younger. Davi grabbed his backpack, wrapped him up in a blanket, and picked him up. He mumbled and stirred as he nestled against her neck, but he didn't wake up. He was accustomed to being moved like this late at night.

"Well, I don't know what to say about it, Mom." Davi started for the door. "I guess I'll try not to get robbed Friday night."

"Can't be no Friday night. Dale and me is going to Wheeling. You're gonna have to find another sitter or you gonna have to change your schedule."

"You know I can't do that."

"You can't keep it up Davida. School, work, and this child just ain't working." Her mom lit another cigarette and turned off the TV. "You're going to have to face the facts, girl."

Davi sighed and opened the door. Alex mewed against her neck, and she shifted his weight. "I'll figure out something else. Thanks for keeping him."

"You can't leave that boy with just anybody," her mom yelled as she watched Davi buckle him into his seat.

"Well, I guess that's no concern of yours. We won't trouble you again." Alex's head flopped over and Davi marveled at how the kid slept through anything.

"That ain't what I meant. I just think you need to face reality."

"Mom. I'm tired. I'm broke, and somebody shot me tonight. I can't with you right now."

"Shot you? What do you mean?" Her mom looked at her frantically.

"Shot at me. At me," Davi said.

Her mom looked at her curiously, then sighed. "Go home. We'll figure it out tomorrow." She stalked back in the house.

Davi slid in the driver's seat and coaxed the Focus to life again. It was a thirty-minute drive to her rattle-trap trailer in the park outside of town. She got Alex inside and pulled off his clothes.

"Mom, I want a wolf. A big one, to ride," he said.

"Well, we can't have pets here, so I guess you'll have to wait on a giant wolf." She pulled the tattered old Star Wars blanket up around his shoulders and he nestled down in his bed.

"I'm getting one," he said. "I dreamed it."

"I dreamed about Ryan Reynolds and a million dollars,"

Davi said. "I hope we both get what we want." She kissed his forehead and turned out the light.

After she'd changed at the restaurant and gotten rid of her burnt, bloody shirt, it was sort of like the whole thing hadn't been real to her. It all came crashing back as she showered. She was bloody as hell. She washed it off, and a red river flowed in the bottom of the little standup trailer shower. She examined the tender pink flesh on her chest. It was sore and still healing—soft, angry, and red. She had been shot. Not shot at. Shot. She should be dead on a slab in the county morgue, and yet here she was, showering at three in the morning in her shitty trailer and wondering how it was that she had come back to life.

CHAPTER 3

"Alex, you have five minutes to finish eating and get dressed," Davi said as she poured her coffee. She was half-awake and would have slept another few hours, but they had no time. She had class, and Alex had to be at school. Unfortunately, the kid was standing in front of the tv in his underwear, eating a Pop Tart and watching a Tom and Jerry cartoon on DVD. The only other article of clothing he had managed was a sock on his left foot.

She threw on sweatpants and sweater, then pulled her hair into a bun. She looked a mess, but she didn't care what anyone in her accounting class had to say about her fashion sense. She took a long drink of coffee and closed her eyes. She had slept about two hours, then Alex crawled in bed with her and kicked her in the kidneys, which made sleep impossible.

"I'm about to start counting," she said loudly, her eyes still closed as she drank her coffee. Alex never voluntarily put clothes on, and he was tired and cranky anyway, so it was about to be a Battle Royale to get him into pants.

"I'm sick today," he said around a mouthful of Pop Tart.

"You don't look sick," Davi said. She finished her coffee and rinsed the cup out in the sink. "One…"

Alex stomped—shaking the whole trailer—and whined in protest. "I *am* sick," he yelled.

"Two…"

He flopped down on the brown micro suede sofa and threw his arm across his eyes dramatically. "I'm sick. I have a fever and my face is all flushed."

She wanted to laugh. One of the most difficult parts about being a parent was not laughing at the shit the kid said—well, that, and dealing with all the puke. Her need to get out the door in the next twenty minutes prevented her from really laughing. "Look, if I get to three, your butt is going to be red too."

"Oh…" Alex jumped up and ran back to his room. She heard a great deal of slamming and stomping, but she knew he was at least finding clothes. He wasn't normally a bear to deal with in the mornings, but he was tired and that always made him a dick. He was seven and she was inclined to cut him some slack, but she had a paper to turn in.

When Alex emerged from his room, he wore a pair of orange tiger striped sweatpants, a purple t-shirt, and his worn-out cowboy boots.

"Come here," she said. "Let me smell your breath." He huffed in her face, and she detected Crest and mouthwash. If he had brushed his teeth, she was willing to deal with funky wardrobe decisions. It wasn't like she herself was haute couture. "Alright. Book bag and let's go." She handed him a lunch bag and ignored his protests about bologna.

Davi tuned out his continual stream of whining as he climbed in the back of the car and strapped himself in, then she coaxed the old car to life again. As it sputtered out of her drive, she noticed the blinds on the trailer next door. Her neighbor peeped out of them at her. He was a weird guy. Bushy red hair and pale. He only came out at night and he stared at her too much. Today, he was staring through the blinds like a nosy old lady, which, she supposed was an accurate description of him.

"Hey, Jerry," Alex yelled out the window and waved.

The blinds shut abruptly.

"How do you know his name?" Davi asked. She didn't remember Alex ever mentioning it before.

"He comes out sometimes. I saw him one night when you made me pick up my bike."

Davi didn't like that. She tried not to let Alex out after dark. The trailer park was not an ideal place for kids, or anyone for that matter, but it was all she could afford. She just tried to keep a low profile and a tight leash on Alex.

"Well, don't bug him," Davi said. "And don't talk to strangers."

"He ain't a stranger," Alex said. "He's Jerry. And he's our neighbor. And he has a Nintendo."

"He isn't a stranger," Davi corrected. "And yes, he is. I don't care what he has. You leave him alone."

Alex huffed and whined the entire twenty-minute drive to his elementary school, and somehow, Davi managed to maintain her calm. She'd felt eerily Zen since the night before. She knew that she should be freaking out; she'd died and come back to life, but there wasn't any panic in her, just a strange, unfamiliar sense of calm.

She didn't suppose there was anything to be done about it. If she wanted answers, she wasn't likely to get them, meaning she didn't know of any experts on coming back from the dead or miraculous healing. Sure, there was the preacher at the church she'd once gone to, but she wouldn't even know how to go about starting that conversation, even if she were so inclined to repair relations with the church.

It was something she supposed she would have to deal with not understanding. She felt fine. Her skin was a little raw and she was a bit sore—exactly like she'd been in a car accident—but otherwise okay.

Her issue was going to be the police. She had the feeling that the Sheriff didn't believe her story. Davi wouldn't have believed her either, so she expected to see more of big Sheriff Newsome. Unaccustomed as she was to be dealing with law enforcement, it unnerved her.

"Have a good day," she said to Alex when she pulled up to

the drop off spot. The old car coughed and wheezed as it exhaled a big puff of white smoke. That got her a few dirty looks from the other moms dropping off kids and the teacher on rider-line duty. Davi ignored them and the urge to flip them all off.

"I don't walk to Gran's?" he asked.

"No. I'll get you this afternoon."

"But I always walk."

"Not always. I don't have to work tonight."

His little face brightened, and he grinned. "Oh, boy. Can we get pizza?"

"After the guff I took this morning?" She gave him a disapproving look.

"I'm sorry, Mommy," he said in a small, sad voice as he made his best attempt at looking apologetic.

It made her want to laugh. Again, not laughing at him was one of the toughest things.

"We'll see. If you stay above the line and I get a good report from Miss Fannon, then maybe. Also, you have to clean your room."

"Aww," he looked dejected at the impossibility of all that.

"Get moving, Sad Sack," Davi laughed. "I love you. Be decent."

"Love you too," he grumbled as he slammed the car door.

She slid into her own class just in time, which was fortunate because she was on her last warning for attendance, and she couldn't afford to fail the class. She was three semesters from her degree, which meant a good job for her, and that meant moving Alex out of the shit stain little town and propelling both on to better lives. She felt her phone vibrate several times indicating a string of text messages. She didn't have to look to know who they were from, and for the first time, her calm started to waiver as her mind ran through who was doing the texting and why.

When the class was over, she checked her phone, and her calm was destroyed. She had twelve texts and two missed calls, all from Brian Hill, Alex's father. Davi dated Brian her first year of college. He was cute, but not smart, which Davi had thought fine at first, then the new wore off and she found herself bored by him. Brian never willing read anything that wasn't a traffic sign, and he could barely do that. They met in a bar when she was on winter break, and by the beginning of her spring semester, she was done with him. She was also pregnant. Faced with that issue, Brian had freaked, but after forty-eight hours, decided he should propose. Davi declined. He then suggested she have an abortion, which she also refused, although if she were honest, she had been on the fence about it until he demanded she have the procedure. She kept the kid, ditched the dad, and hadn't regretted either decision in the last six years.

Davi told herself she wouldn't need him at all. She even thought that she could stay in school, but when Alex was born, she hadn't been able to make it work, time-wise or financially, so she put school on hold and got a job. It had been a rough few years, working shitty jobs, scrambling to make ends meet, and never quite succeeding, but she'd found a way to get back in school. The problem was, it required a certain amount of help from both her mother, who was not exactly enamored of the idea of being a grandmother, and Brian, who was equally repelled at the reality of being a father. He was inconsistent with child support and even less consistent with his visitation. Six months earlier, they had a come-to-Jesus meeting where Davi assured him that he would pitch in with childcare or he would pitch in with his full required child support payments. He balked at both, but Davi threatened a formal proceeding, and Brian, terrified of the concept of wage garnishment that Davi described to him, agreed to babysit his own child on weekends.

Brian's numerous texts and calls were to inform her that he was going to be unable to pick up Alex on Saturday, which was bad, because Davi had been counting on Brian to take Alex on Friday, since her mom was bailing on babysitting. She knew he would be pissed if she showed up at his job, but there was no other way to corner him. She had a break between her morning class and her afternoon biology lab, so she climbed in the old car and drove down to the machine shop where Brian worked. When she got there, his truck was there, but he wasn't. He was hiding somewhere in the warren of pipe and sheet metal.

His coworkers laughed as she strode in looking for him. She cornered his friend, Steve.

"Where is he?"

Steve laughed. "Uh oh, Davi. What's got you riled?"

"None of your business. Tell me where he is."

She crossed her arms and stared at him. Davi was small, all of five-foot six, but she was solid and had oddly strong biceps from years of hauling Alex around. Steve was six-three but after looking at her face, he stopped laughing and pointed to the office. "He's in there."

She stalked over to the office and yanked the door open. It was a mess of greasy invoices and shop packets. A Playboy Playmate calendar hung on the wall. The man that owned the shop, Charlie Gordon, was a fat, gross pig. All four hundred pounds of him strained the cheap office chair to its limit. He sat at his desk amid a pile of Funyons and chewed a bite from a thick bologna sandwich. A glop of mayonnaise clung to his chin. He didn't look up from the porn he was watching on his computer.

"Where is he, Charlie?"

"Hiding' in the shitter," Charlie said, his mouth full of Wonder Bread and bologna.

"Sounds about right," Davi said. She eyeballed the door to the restroom. It had likely been white once, but it was now a dingy grey. The area around the door handle was black with filth. She hesitated before she grabbed it, but then committed fully, turned the knob, and opened the door.

Brian wasn't using the toilet. He stood there glowering at her. Davi couldn't control the disgust she felt. She gagged. The bathroom was the filthiest place she had ever seen, with black handprints everywhere from men who didn't wash. There was a stack of nudie magazines next to the toilet and the room stank of shit—she assumed it smelled of that perpetually—and a man's asshole, dank and meaty. How Brian could stomach being in there only to hide, Davi had no idea. Her opinion of him sunk even lower, and she had thought that an impossibility.

"You're such a chicken shit," she said to him as she tried not to breathe through her nose.

"Davi, what the fuck?" He tried to look offended but couldn't pull it off.

"Get out of there Brian. I don't have all day." She motioned him out. His body language was almost precisely the same as his son's had been earlier in the morning, and he stomped out of the filthy restroom, then out into the machine shop.

Davi followed him and tried not to think about how much Alex looked like him. It didn't endear Brian to her, it made her sad. "You're taking Alex Friday night." She didn't waste any time.

"No, I'm fucking not," he said. "I told you I got to work Saturday."

She knew that he didn't have to work. None of the morons at the shop ever voluntarily worked past three on Fridays. They all went out to the Misty and got plastered.

"No, you have to pick up your kid. *I* have to work."

He began blustering and protesting.

Davi shook her head "Look, you agreed to this. I made my schedule. It's done."

"It ain't done, Davida. It ain't done until I say it's done." He crossed his arms. "I got to work Saturday. I can't take him."

"Get your mom or your sister to watch him then, but you're taking him."

"Mom is out of town and Lacey is busy."

"I doubt all that. And I could just go ask Charlie if you're working."

"Go on ask him. He'll tell you we're working overtime."

Davi rolled her eyes, then nodded. "Have it your way." She went back in the office. "Is Brian working overtime Saturday?"

"Fuck no," Charlie said. He still hadn't looked up from the porn.

"Got it," Davi said as she saluted him. She walked calmly back to Brian. "He says he didn't approve any overtime."

"Fuckin'… well I can't take him Davida. I won't." He picked up a piece of pipe and threw it down. It clanged loudly on the concrete floor. Davi didn't budge.

"Look, I do not care what backwoods hill skank you have lined up to bang all weekend, you have a responsibility to deal with your son. I cut you enough slack, Brian. You don't want to pay child support, and I haven't pushed it, but I gotta work this weekend, and I have to study in between that, so you are going to take him."

"The only backwoods hill skank I ever banged was you," he said, his eyes narrowed, dark and mean.

Davi laughed out loud. "Even if it were true, that wouldn't sting."

Brian reached out and grabbed her arm. He clamped on to her and squeezed. "I'm telling you, Davida—"

Davi looked down at her arm. He was squeezing it hard enough to leave a mark, probably a bruise later. She could see the tendons in his forearm straining, but she couldn't feel it. It was a slight feeling of pressure, as if she had an elastic sleeve against her skin, like he was hardly squeezing at all. She reached out calmly and grabbed his arm, meaning to simply remove his grasp. He screamed when she touched him. She wasn't squeezing or exerting any pressure at all. "What the hell is wrong with you, Brian?"

He started crying and dropped to his knees. She still held his arm. He was beet red and sweat poured from him. His mouth opened to form words but then he closed it, his lips white and thin. He pressed them tightly together. She barely tightened her grip on his arm, and he opened his mouth, spittle flecking from the corners as he spoke in a half-whisper, half-cry.

"I-I can't watch him because every Saturday night I go to Charleston to that gay bar. I meet a guy there and we go to a hotel and he fucks me all weekend. I been doing it for the last six months, and I love it."

Davi let go of his arm, and he started vomiting. His arm was red. A clear imprint of her hand remained where she touched him, as if her grip had burned his skin. He vomited yellow bile until he lay spent and empty on the shop floor. She knew without a doubt in her mind that he had told her the truth.

It wasn't that she had always suspected he was gay— she hadn't really considered it—but she knew that he couldn't make up something like that. He didn't have the world view or the creativity. He had always expressed the same casual disgust for gay men that most of the men she knew had— maybe a bit less actually—but she knew that he wouldn't lie or joke about it.

But it was more than that. Davi *knew*. She was one hundred percent certain that Brian had just told her his deepest, darkest, most terrifying secret, and she was also one hundred percent certain that she had made him. She just knew it, like she knew the sky was blue. It was fact.

The acidic smell of his bile hit her, and she was jerked back in to the reality of the situation. She looked down at him, then took a step backward. "I'm… Brian—"

He looked up at her as he held his arm, his face panicked and terrified. "Why… why did I say… what did you do to me?"

"I don't know. I didn't mean to do anything. You just… you just—"

He got to his feet, wobbled, and puked again. "Go. I'll pay you. I'll do whatever. Don't ever touch me again."

He sniffed and cried a bit more, then wiped his face on his arm. "What am I going to do?"

"Calm down. I'm the only one that heard you. I don't give a shit if you let the whole Pittsburgh Steelers football team fuck you. I just need you to watch your son this weekend."

He nodded. "I'll… I'll take him." He looked at her and his face was so sad and frightened. He looked exactly like Alex after he had a nightmare. Davi sighed.

"Look, just… just never freaking mind, ok?" She knew he was wrecked, and even though she knew she was going to have a hell of a time trying to figure out how to work and deal with Alex, she knew she didn't want to leave Alex with him. It wasn't that the secret gay thing bothered her. She now sensed a sincere stability problem and didn't think Brian could handle it.

"Don't turn me in or hurt me again, Davi. I'll pay you some this weekend."

"I'm not going to have you arrested, and I won't hurt you. I didn't do anything to you, Brian." She was lying. Davi knew exactly what she had done to him. His arm looked terrible. The gigantic bruise formed fast and Davi saw it swell. She had barely touched him. She knew he would rather die than press charges and admit that a woman had fucked him up. He'd already admitted to being gay. Davi didn't think he could survive admitting that she had almost ripped his arm off and made him cry like a five-year-old. "Go out back and clean yourself up. Tell them I kicked you in the balls if they ask about the puke." She didn't know what else to say, and while she didn't want to hurt him, she really wasn't all that sorry, just confused.

She left him wiping his face in the shop. When she got back behind the wheel of the Focus, she felt the eerie sense of calm and control return to her. She had no childcare, would likely lose her job, and had nearly ripped off her ex's arm while forcing him to come out of the closet. As she made her way to her biology lab, she decided life couldn't get much weirder. Later, she was surprised at how wrong she was about that.

CHAPTER 4

Don't slam the car door," Davi yelled. Alex ignored her and slammed the door of the Focus so hard it shook the glass. She had her hands full with her books and the pizza box. He did remember to hold the door to the trailer open for her. That was an improvement from the norm.

"Go pick all the clothes up off your floor," Davi said, pointing back the hallway to his bedroom. "Now. No TV until you do it."

Alex started to throw a fit. "But I'm starving," he whined as he stamped his feet and jumped around.

I can pretty much guarantee you are not," Davi said dryly. "It will take you five minutes if you shut your cake hole and go do it."

"No, it won't. It will take forever, and I will die," Alex cried, but he headed back to his room.

Highly unlikely," she said. She set the pizza in the middle of the table. She cleaned up briefly, then headed down the hallway to her own room. On the way back, she stopped in and saw that Alex had cleared his floor of all the clothes. He did have a scattering of Hot Wheels on the floor, but he had done what she asked about the clothes. "Ok. Pizza. Then homework."

"I don't have any," he yelled as he sprinted down the hall and attacked the pizza.

"I think you're fibbing to me," she said. Davi managed to snag one piece of pizza, and she ate it standing up. She jumped when the doorbell rang. Nobody ever rang the doorbell. It was a trailer. She hadn't even known there was doorbell. She was cautious, but when she opened the door, it was only the fat, pasty neighbor.

"Oh, umm, hey." He looked nervous. He shifted from foot to foot and made exaggerated hand gestures. She had a feeling this was one of the only times he had ever conversed with a female. He had that strange, anti-social look about him, skittish and hunched. His burnt-red hair was an unruly curly mop, but not a cute unruly mop, more like a literal unruly mop. He was dumpy. She didn't guess she would have called him fat, exactly, more like doughy and flabby. His face was pasty pale without even a hint of a red spot, which she thought odd. She had never seen a redhead who had such strange uncolored skin without even a broken vein on the nose. She couldn't see any redness on him, not anywhere.

"Hey yourself," Davi replied. She didn't invite him in. She stared.

"I just wanted to bring you this." He awkwardly handed her a bunch of mail, almost dropping it as he tried to keep the flyers and store ads together. It was all junk, the weekly ads and offers for collectible plates that nobody cared about.

She took the offered stack of papers. "Thanks," Davi said.

It was weird behavior. It wasn't like that was the mail that mattered if it got delivered to a different box by mistake. He didn't go away. He just stood at the door, staring.

"Yeah, umm... sure. Wouldn't want you to miss the coupons." He laughed a high-pitched, snorting laugh.

"Be a real shame," Davi nodded.

"Oh, umm... my name is Jerry. Jerry Monroe. I, I uh... live next trailer over." He held out his hand.

Davi looked down at his pale, pudgy hand, then at him. "Davida Barker." She shook his hand. It was soft and smooth, like a woman's. It was also cold. Not clammy or slightly wet, just cold.

He grimaced when she shook his hand. "Oh, wow, you got a firm grip," he said. He looked her over curiously and inhaled deeply. She could have sworn that he was smelling her.

"Ok, yeah. Thanks, there, ah, Jerry," she said. "We're kind of eating and doing homework so..."

"Oh, yeah. Sure then..." He still just stood there staring at her.

At that point, Alex poked his head around her and smiled

wide with his mouth full of pizza. "Hey Jerry!" Davi looked down at him, confused.

Jerry smiled at Alex and gave him a little wave. "Hey Alex. How's it going?"

"Pretty good. We got pizza. Want a piece? Come on in—"

"Alex," Davi growled.

"Thanks, but um… I can't eat pizza," Jerry laughed. He shrugged at Davi. "We met a couple weeks ago. I got a new Nintendo."

"So I heard. Look, Jerry, you can't just invite my kid inside your house." Davi bristled.

"Oh, well, he didn't come in. He saw me with the box, and we started talking."

"Yeah, well, either way." Davi was relieved that Alex hadn't gone inside the weirdo's house, but she knew that wouldn't last, not with the lure of video games. Alex didn't have any and the kids in his class were all crazy for them.

"Mom, he has a Nintendo and I don't." Alex picked up her annoyance.

"Go eat and do your homework," Davi said, shoving Alex back inside.

He protested, but she gave him her best death stare and he went back to the table. She could hear him grumbling.

"I wouldn't ever hurt him," Jerry said.

"Yeah? Well that's what I'm sure people who hurt little boys say too," Davi sighed. "Look, no offense or anything but I don't know you and I don't want him hanging out in your trailer, okay?"

"No, no, I get it. But, you know, I wouldn't… okay." He held his fat, smooth hands up and smiled. "Fair enough. We're neighbors though, so if you need help, just knock."

"We've lived here a year. You were here when we got here." She folded her arms over her chest. Why was he so set on being neighborly suddenly? She had seen him staring out his blinds at them and the idiot across the street who laid out to tan in her plain underwear. If he wanted to be helpful, he could have made a move before now.

"Yeah, but I'm just trying to get to know people a little," he said.

She smelled a lie.

"Ok, well, cool. Thanks for the mail. Take care."

She shut the door, then sat down at the table. Alex had eaten four pieces of pizza and was working on a fifth.

"Guess I'm lucky to get any," Davi said. She took another piece but gave the last to him.

"Why were you mean to him?" Alex asked.

"I wasn't mean to him."

"Yes you were. He's nice. He has a Nintendo." Alex shoved the entire crust in his mouth.

"Hey, don't be a gross pig. Manners. Just because somebody has a Nintendo doesn't mean they're nice."

Alex finished chewing and attacked his last piece. "Well he was nice to me. He said I could play sometime if you said I could."

"Not happening," Davi said. She opened her biology book and started reading.

"Mom. I never have any fun." He slid down in his chair and started crying the whining fake tears that she hated.

"You're hard up, for sure," she said evenly, ignoring him.

He got up and stomped back the hallway with the pizza still in hand.

"Hey! No food back there. Get back here." She didn't look up from the book. He knew better than to take food back to his room. There had been an incident with a bowl of cereal once. Davi had almost puked when she found it.

He kicked the paneling, which made a sad vibrating hollow sound, then stomped back to the table. He finished his pizza as he cried.

"You're doing your homework, then bath, then bed. No toys tonight."

"I don't even have any toys," Alex said as he flopped his head down on the table and hid his face.

"Oh my God. Alex. Not tonight." She got up and pulled his homework out of his book bag. "Get it done. Now. Stop crying and being a butthole."

He looked up at her and laughed through his tears. "You said butthole."

She looked down at him and his goofy smile. He was seven and went from Apocalyptic meltdown over cheese to laughing at farts and buttholes in ten seconds. She kissed him. "You're really lucky I love you." She handed him his big fat pencil. "Math problems. Do them."

He liked math, so he threw himself into his worksheet.

She did her biology homework. He scooted closer to her as they worked until he was leaning against her.

Her mind wandered from mitosis and meiosis. She thought about everything that had happened in the last twenty-four hours. She had died. That was a fact. And she was different. She didn't know how, but that was also fact. Those things bothered her, and would continue to do so, but what bothered her more was the realization that she had come remarkably close to leaving the little pizza-eating weirdo cuddled against her alone in the world. That prospect was more terrifying to her than any of the rest of it. She tried to put it out of her mind, along with the other things that she didn't have the capacity to understand now, including why Jerry Monroe was suddenly so interested in being neighborly. That was the least of her issues and would wait for another day.

CHAPTER 5

FRIDAY MORNING, Davi woke up with Alex's feet in her face. He stretched across the Queen-sized bed with his own blanket over him and on top of hers. She rolled over to get the toes out of her face but refused to get up. Her alarm still had twenty minutes. She had nobody to watch Alex for the weekend. She couldn't leave him, and her mom was gone. She and her boyfriend Dale had left for Wheeling already. Davi ran through her options where babysitters were concerned. She had nobody. Nobody free anyway, and she couldn't afford to pay. The rent was due, and she didn't quite have all of it put back. Davi was counting on her shifts this weekend to make up the difference. It was looking grim for that plan.

She had no classes during the day, so she was hopeful to find a miracle before her shift started at four. Why she was hopeful, she had no idea. She had even thought better of Brian and texted him, but he ignored her. When she called the machine shop, Charlie cussed her out and told her Brian was a deadbeat who hadn't shown up to work.

Her last option would be to call Brian's mother, Sherri, and see if she would take Alex for the weekend. Sherri despised Davi, and Davi despised her right back. Davi hated her because she was a thundercunt who babied Brian and threatened to have Alex taken from Davi, despite Brian being unfit to raise a goldfish, let alone a kid. Sherri hated Davi just because, and had from the first. None of that family ever cared about Alex unless it was Christmas or Easter. They started calling in early December wanting Alex for Christmas Eve. She understood. It was fun to dress him up and watch his face as he opened presents. The problem was, they only cared once a year, and Alex didn't know them well enough not to cry when she left him with them. That ruined Sherri's perfect Christmas Eve, and Davi was summoned to pick Alex up early. After that, she refused their requests, which would make it difficult to ask a favor now.

Her alarm went off, and she and Alex grumbled in harmony. He had as much love for mornings as she did, which was none. Davi hit snooze on her phone, and Alex rustled around until he was on her open side and cuddled against her, with his head on her heart. She wrapped her arms around him and tried not to think about all the complications.

If she called off, she was done. Fired, for sure, and it

wasn't like there was a plethora of jobs in town. She could go work at the IGA. She hated Skippy Bowman, though. He looked at her boobs every time she went in there and still managed to sneer at her EBT card when she used it. Some of the other girls that worked at the restaurant had worked at the IGA before and they told stories about him. She guessed she would do what she had to do, but she hoped it would be a last resort. Davi was tired. She was tired of always having to have a last resort.

Alex snuggled closer and mewed like a kitten, then yawned. "I don't feel good," he murmured, then buried his face against her neck.

"Sounds perfectly normal to me." She laughed and kissed his ear. "It's Friday. You like Fridays."

"Oh yeah," he nodded, and she felt him smile against her skin. "We get pizza today and extra recess."

"Yep. So let's go. Breakfast. Clothes. Teeth." She gave him a last squeeze and patted his little butt.

He gave a little protest, but the lure of school pizza and an extra recess was too much for him, so he climbed out of bed when she did and headed to the bathroom.

As she ate her cereal, her phone rang. She didn't recognize the number, so she ignored it. It rang two more times. On the third call, she picked it up and was sorry she did.

It was the big sheriff. He had a few more questions for her and wanted her to come in at ten to talk. Davi wanted to refuse. She thought she remembered that she could refuse, but then thought the refusal would look worse, so she agreed. When she hung up, her mood was dark and worried. Alex noticed.

"What's wrong Mom?" he asked as he slurped his milk.

"Nothing. Clothes. Teeth."

Her tone was sufficiently serious, so he didn't test her. He emerged with ten minutes to spare, dressed in his best Star Wars T-shirt and his hair spiked up with an inordinate amount of hair gel.

It made her laugh and shook her slightly out of her worried funk. She guessed Fridays were fancy.

He kissed her cheek when she dropped him at school.

"Have a good day, Mommy." He grinned at her and her heart just about burst.

"Later Nerd. I love you. Be decent." She almost cried. He turned and waved at her before he went inside. He never did that. Davi shook off the hinky feeling and decided to go to the grocery store before going home.

The IGA had just opened and was devoid of customers. She picked up a gallon of milk and a three-pack of macaroni and cheese, food for the weekend. The clerk rolled her eyes and made a disapproving clicking sound when Davi paid with her EBT card. The card didn't have quite enough on it and Davi had to finish paying with change from her car console.

"It spends the same, you hateful twat," an annoyed woman's voice said from behind her.

Davi turned and looked for the speaker. It was a tall blonde woman with a grumpy expression on her pretty face.

The woman stared daggers at the cashier as she set a box of Frosted Flakes and a half-gallon of Almond Milk down on the belt. The cashier huffed as if she was about to say something, but the blonde woman narrowed her eyes.

"Think real careful about what you say next," the woman said. She pointed to Davi, then back to the cashier. "If you was smart, the next words out of your mouth would be an apology directed at her."

"Yeah, no, that's okay. She don't need to apologize," Davi said. She could feel the anger coming in waves off the blonde. The muscles in the woman's arms flexed, and Davi could see them ripple through the thin grey sweatshirt the woman wore.

"No, it ain't okay. Money is money, and anyway, she ain't no different than you. She thinks it, though. She ain't never had to use grub stubs, so she thinks she's better."

"You don't have to apologize," Davi said to the cashier. "I'm good." She picked up her plastic bag and nodded politely at the blonde.

"Be seeing you," the woman said as Davi walked away. Davi tuned and looked back at her. It was an odd thing to say. The blonde didn't look up as she paid and Davi went about her business.

Davi started the Focus, which sputtered and choked, then stalled out.

"Aww… come on. Not today," she said as she cranked the key again and prayed for the decrepit engine to start. It refused, and Davi felt herself start down that path to an ugly hysterical cry as the weight of the day came rushing down upon her. She pounded the steering wheel and sobbed.

"Your car is a piece of shit," a voice said through the glass. Davi jumped.

"Jesus. You scared me," she said as she looked up.

The blonde stood outside the window. She motioned for Davi to roll the window down. "Didn't mean to. That thing is done."

"It can't be," Davi said. She got out of the car, ignored the blonde, and opened the hood. She wasn't sure what was wrong but was an old hand at whacking on stuff inside the engine and getting it to start one more time. Davi used the box wrench she kept handy to beat on the alternator a few times.

"That ain't gonna do anything," the blonde said in an amused tone.

"You don't know this car," Davi said. She got back in and tried to start it again. It sputtered and whined, then died. "Son of a Bitch!" Davi yelled. She got out and whacked a few other things. She doubted that would help, but it made her feel slightly better.

"I had a truck just like it once," the blonde woman said. "When they go, they go. I'll give you a ride to wherever you need."

Davi looked at the woman and couldn't tell if she was hitting on her or not. It was better to be safe than sorry. "That's okay. I'll call somebody."

The blonde looked at her and smiled. "If I was you, I'd be

thinking the same thing, believe me. I don't mean no harm. I promise."

That was the second time in two days she had heard somebody say that to her. "People keep saying that, and I can't help but think that's exactly what people who want to do harm would say."

The blonde woman cocked her head and looked Davi over carefully. "You ain't got no idea who I am, do you?"

"No," Davi said as she looked through her phone for somebody, anybody she could call at eight-thirty in the morning who could pick her up. "Should I?" Davi looked up at the woman.

The woman's face got very dark and contemplative. "It's a feather in your cap that you don't," she said. She seemed to shake herself and give a low growl, which made Davi stare for a second, and added a bit of worry into her brain.

"Okay, well, I mean, thanks, but I'll call somebody and get them to help me. Cops will, I guess." She said the last more as an idea to herself.

"No. We ain't gonna involve them at all," the blonde said.

"What?" Davi stared at her, confused. Her heart began to race as she sensed danger.

"I got a garage. I'm gonna call a wrecker and have them come get this junker. We'll take a look and fix it if we can. You can come with me and wait while they work on it. We got business."

"Us? I don't know you and I'm not going with you." Davi backed away.

"Easy there, kid. If I wanted to hurt you, I would have. I need you to help me out, and maybe I can help you too." The blonde held her hands up and smiled.

Davi took a deep breath and regarded her. She was bigger than Davi. She was clearly stronger—Davi could see the muscles. And she had a no-fucking-around attitude. Davi knew lots of hood girls like that in high school. She didn't remember this one, but whether she was older or younger, Davi couldn't tell. The woman had an unlined babyface but also a look of immense responsibility and an almost care-worn appearance that rumbled just below the high cheek-bones and beautiful skin. She was dangerous, like a predatory animal in a pretty package. Based on that, she should have run the other direction, but a look in the woman's eyes made her stay. The pretty brown eyes were sad, not dangerous. There was deep, ingrained sorrow in them, and Davi had the feeling that they had once been kind but now were clouded by heaps of trouble.

"Kid, look, please? I promise, no harm will come to you. But I don't want you talking to the Sheriff, and I'm bettin' you don't wanna do that either. So let's just help each other out. Come with me. I'll fix everything." The woman held her hand out. "Please?"

Davi looked at the hand. She looked back up at the big brown eyes and saw what she had sensed earlier, sad mixed with kind, despite the hard exterior. She sighed audibly and put her hand in the blonde's. "Okay, but I can't pay for the car."

"I don't care about that right now." The blonde led her over to an immaculately clean black Jeep and opened the door for her.

Davi climbed in. When the blonde got in, Davi asked, "Who are you?"

"Delilah Monroe," the woman answered as she started the Jeep and pulled out of the IGA parking lot.

Davi swallowed hard and her heart raced. She had just gotten into a vehicle, going God knows where with the head of the criminal underworld of Denton County. Her strange life had somehow gotten even stranger, and she lamented the decision to get out of bed at all.

CHAPTER 6

"Want a Coke or something?" Delilah Monroe offered up a can of soda.

"No thank you," Davi said.

When Davi realized who she had gotten into the vehicle with, she had visions of being spirited away to a seedy crime shack back up in a holler somewhere, a place she might never get out of. In truth, Delilah had driven into town, to a quiet block of offices. Her office appeared to be in plain sight right in the center of town, not in a meth shack on a mountain top.

The office was comfortable. Modern, but warm, which was at once odd and yet perfectly in character with what Davi had sensed so far. There was a big solid wood desk and matching office chairs, but after Delilah offered her the soda, she motioned for Davi to have a seat in a fat leather chair.

Delilah sat down casually on the matching leather sofa. The chair was soft and over-stuffed. It was genuine leather, not the plastic fake stuff and probably cost more money than Davi had ever seen at one time.

Delilah crossed her legs, popped the top on the Coke, and sipped it. "So, the Sheriff wants to talk to you about that business at Applebee's the other night."

Davi tried to look like she didn't know what the words of the question meant but failed. "I guess so."

The blonde laughed. "Davida, I doubt you guess at much."

"Okay, so what do you want with me? I don't know anything. I didn't do anything, and I sure as hell don't want to talk to that big sheriff, so I really don't understand why you care about me at all."

"What are you?" Delilah leaned over and looked at her carefully. She sniffed long, not bothering to try and disguise it as Jerry had done.

"What kind of question is that?" Davi asked. She backed into the chair, as far away as she could get.

"You had you some trouble the other night, right?"

"Yeah. Some white trash robbed us." Davi shrugged. That was already in the paper. Old news.

"He did more than that." Delilah sat back on the sofa.

"Shot at me. He was so tweaked he missed."

Delilah shook her head. "He shot you point blank in the chest. Killed you dead, yet here you sit."

Davi's stomach plummeted. "That's not possible."

"Kid, a lot of shit ain't possible. I've seen all kinds of shit that ain't possible. That word don't hardly mean nothing."

"If somebody shot me in the chest, I would have died."

Delilah nodded. "Most people, sure." She pointed at Davi. "You don't appear to be most people."

When Davi didn't respond, Delilah went on.

"So, the fucking idiot that shot you and took your money, well, at one point, he worked for me." She held up her hands apologetically. "He freelanced that dumb robbery. That ain't my business model."

"I mean, okay?" Davi said. She had no idea where any of this was going.

"Hold on." Delilah made a call on her phone. "Yeah. Now."

"Now what?" Davi asked. She had a panicked feeling and started to get up from the chair.

"Sit down, kid."

"Stop calling me kid. I'm not a kid."

"You are, but okay. Sit down, Davi."

"How did you know that name?"

"It ain't hard to figure out. Davida is long and it don't suit you."

"You can tell that from knowing me for thirty minutes?" Davi scoffed.

"Kid, I knew that from knowing you thirty seconds."

Davi rolled her eyes.

"Hey, look, I got one of them names too."

Davi nodded. "I suppose you do. Delilah."

"It's just Del. Make it easy on us."

"I don't know why I'd want to make it easy on the person who kidnapped me."

"I'm fixing your car. After we figure out what's what, you're free to go. You got a kid to worry over."

"How the fuck do you know about my kid?" Davi stood up, suddenly angry. She balled her fists up. Big bad ass crime boss or not, Davi wasn't going to let Alex be any part of it.

Del stood up, and Davi realized how much bigger Del was. Del was six feet to Davi's five and a half, and strong. Her muscles twitched and rippled when she stood. She looked every bit that big, dangerous animal that Davi had originally seen in the IGA.

Davi didn't back down, though. She stood as tall as she could. She felt the hair on the back of her neck stand up and a buzzing of energy in her hands.

Del's eyes narrowed. She growled and bared her teeth. Davi let the energy dissipate, and when she did, Del calmed.

"I'll ask again, what are you?" Del's voice was calm and quiet.

"Honestly, I don't know anymore." Davi sat down on the chair and tears welled up in her eyes.

Del looked as if she meant to comfort her but stopped herself. She sat back down on the sofa. "Believe it or not, I understand how you feel."

Davi nodded. Whatever she had just seen from Del suggested that Del was different too—not the same different as Davi but not like everyone else in the world.

Just then, the door opened and two huge, burly guys with

well-manicured beards and hipster gentleman haircuts came in dragging a squirming mess wearing a black hood. The man was trussed up. His ankles and knees were bound and so were his hands and arms. They plopped him down in one of the desk chairs, and he immediately tried to get up but fell over because his feet were bound.

"What a fucking idiot," Del said. She got up and kicked the man viciously in the ribs. "Settle the fuck down Andrew." She motioned for the men to put him back in the chair. They did, then removed the hood. He blinked and his eyes darted wildly around the room. Davi knew him at once. He was the man who shot her.

Del looked at Davi's wide eyes and panicked expression. "Easy, Davi. He ain't gonna do shit to you."

Davi nodded but her heart still pounded.

"He's the one who attacked you, yes?"

Davi nodded. "He did."

Del walked over and ripped the duct tape off Andrew's mouth. He screamed as it took off big swaths of his nasty, patchy facial hair.

"Andrew. You owe this young lady an apology."

"Del... please. She ain't right." Andrew strained at his bonds and his wide eyes focused on Davi.

"You're scared of her? You weren't scared of her when you fucking shot her and took her work money." She slapped Andrew hard, and his head snapped back with more force that Davi would have thought possible.

"You best forget about her and be scared of me," Del said.

"One, you know the rules. We don't steal from this town. And two, you did shit without my say."

He looked at her and nodded. "I'm real sorry, Del. Real sorry. Won't happen again." He began to cry. "Please?"

Del patted him on the shoulder and nodded. "Tell Davi you're sorry for hurting her."

He looked at Davi and kept crying. "I seen it Del. She ain't human."

Davi watched as Del dug her fingers into Andrew's shoulder. She heard the bones break and pop. Andrew screamed for all he was worth.

"I-I-I'm sorry," he screamed.

Del nodded. "That's better. Thank you." She let go of him and walked around to the desk. She pulled a small caliber handgun from the drawer. "So, Andrew. You shot Davi, right in the chest. That's what you told Jimmy." Del looked over at one of the guys, Jimmy, who nodded.

"Yes. I shot her. She should have died," Andrew said.

"Well, it wasn't nice to kill her. She's got a kid. We don't fucking do shit like that." Del walked calmly between Davi and Andrew. "You're sure you shot her? You didn't miss? You wasn't fucking high or nothing?"

Andrew shook his head. "No. I wasn't on nothing. Okay, a little crank, but just a little. I wasn't tweaking."

Del nodded. "Okay. Okay, so you shot her." She looked at Davi. "He shot you?"

Davi swallowed hard and nodded. Before Davi could register what was happening, Del took the gun and pointed at her. It wasn't the deafening roar of the big handgun from the other night, but more like a firecracker pop. When Davi looked down, there was another hole in her chest. The charred flesh around it smoked, and blood burbled up from it. Davi stared down at it but stayed upright. The hole rippled and shimmered as the flesh started to mend itself. In just a few seconds, the wound healed. Her chest was whole again, just like before. She hadn't felt anything but a little pressure and sting.

She looked over at Del incredulously. "You shot me."

Del looked unconcerned. She shrugged and nodded. "I did. And you didn't die." She looked over at Andrew who looked terrified. He struggled against his bonds and sobbed. "Looks like you was telling the truth, shitbag. For once in your miserable life." Del pointed the gun at Andrew's head and shot him. His brains flew out all over the mahogany desk and he slumped backward.

Del put the gun back in the desk drawer, then grabbed a sweater from a closet and handed it to Davi. Her sweatshirt was burnt and ruined.

"Sorry I shot you. You want a job?"

CHAPTER 7

DAVI PULLED the sweater over her head. She was still humming and buzzing from the gunshot wound. She felt fine, but it was like everything was in slow motion. Davi remembered that feeling was because of adrenaline, but while she felt alert, Davi was having trouble connecting real thoughts together. All she could think about was being shot and watching Andrew's head explode all over the office.

Del was looking at her and saying something. Davi was unable to discern the meaning of the words, but she squinted her eyes and concentrated. When she finally understood the question, she looked at Del as if she had three heads.

"You shot me. Why would I take a job with you?"

Del laughed. "Get over it, kid. I didn't mean nothing by it. Wasn't personal."

"I'd say shooting somebody is pretty damn personal,

Delilah." Davi started for the door. "Fuck your job and double fuck you."

Del moved quicker than Davi had ever seen a human move before, and suddenly, she was between Davi and the door. She leaned casually against the frame, crossed her arms, and tilted her head at Davi as she smiled a cold smile.

"Number one. It wasn't personal. There was no other way to tell if Andrew was telling the truth about you. Number two, I'm sorry I scared you, but I ain't sorry we know. And number three, don't call me Delilah."

Del's tone was calm and low, but serious. Davi didn't nod or acknowledge anything. Her heart pounded. She couldn't say she wasn't scared of Del—she was, as clearly this woman would do whatever she had to do—but looking at Del, Davi also knew that Del was telling her the truth.

"If you had been wrong, my kid—"

"Well, I wasn't wrong, but if I had been, that kid would have been taken care of right."

"Without his mom? How you figure that's right?"

Del shrugged. "Things are tough all over for lots of kids. I'da made certain things was as easy as possible for him, even without his mama."

"You must have a fucked-up sense of parents if you think that would be okay," Davi said.

Del nodded. "Kid, that's a fact."

"Look, you found out what you wanted to find out. Can I just go?"

Del looked her up and down for a few seconds. "I know

you ain't gonna rat me out to the Sheriff. You think you might wanna do that, you best think again."

"Why would I? How could I explain any of this without landing in jail myself?" Davi rolled her eyes. She supposed she could give evidence against Del. She had seen her shoot the man in cold blood and not so much as bat an eyelash. But while she couldn't hurt Davi—at least she didn't think she could hurt her—Del could hurt other people in Davi's life.

"That's smart thinking, Davida. Very smart. Look, we got no beef. I'm sorry I popped you one and scared you. Had to be done. I'm serious about the job. You get sick of slinging boneless wings, you let me know." Del motioned to one of the big guys. "Jimmy will take you home."

"Just give me my car back," Davi said. "I don't need anything else from you."

"Fair enough. We'll send it out to your place directly. Go with Jimmy." Del opened the door and gave a little half-bow. "Have a nice afternoon."

Davi shook her head as she walked through the door and down the steps to Jimmy's big black truck. She wasn't sure what had just happened, but one thing she was quite sure of was that neither she nor Delilah Monroe believed their business to be finished.

CHAPTER 8

JIMMY DELIVERED Davi to her trailer without saying a single word. That was fine with Davi. She figured the less she said to anyone in a hillbilly crime syndicate, the better, but she wished he might have given her some hope that she would get her vehicle back.

He said nothing. He stared straight ahead the whole time, and Davi sensed he was afraid of her. She thought that was funny. She had seen them murder a man, and yet they were afraid of her. She couldn't do anything to them.

Well, she didn't think she could do anything to them, but she wasn't entirely sure about that. Maybe she could do to him what she had done to Brian. The problem was, she didn't know exactly how she had done that.

At any rate, Jimmy had been polite enough. He dropped her off at her trailer and didn't bother her at all. Davi slammed his truck door closed and stalked up the steps. She yanked off the sweater and tossed it in the trash. If it was Delilah Monroe's, she didn't want anything to do with it.

Davi showered. As she rubbed soap into her chest, she realized the skin felt tender. It was fresh and new as a baby's and slightly raw. The gunshot hadn't hurt exactly. There had been pressure and a tingly stinging sensation—like when you have a foot wake up after it falls asleep on you. It was uncomfortable, but not exactly painful. It had felt more annoying than anything else. Once again, by some miracle, she was alive and whole. She had no explanation.

By one o'clock, her car had not been returned. She had to pick Alex up at three and be at work by four, both of which were impossible without her vehicle. If she was honest with herself, going to work was going to be impossible altogether. She had no options lined up for babysitting Alex. She'd have to call off work. That would be bad news for her for sure.

By two o'clock, she started to panic. Picking Alex up was a priority, but she had no way to do that. Brian was still not answering his phone, and her pleading voicemails and texts to just go and pick Alex up from school and bring him to her were ignored. She slammed the phone down on the table. So much for the word of Delilah Monroe. She was out a vehicle and a job.

Davi was on the verge of calling a cab to take her to pick up Alex when she heard the crunch of gravel outside the trailer. She ran to the window and looked outside. Her brow creased in confusion when a black Honda Civic pulled up in her driveway. It wasn't brand new, but it wasn't an old one either, and it was immaculately clean. Her confusion turned to rage when Delilah Monroe stepped out of it. Davi yanked the trailer door open and stood on the little porch, hands on her hips.

"Where's my car?"

"I told you that thing was done for," Del said. She walked over to the porch and held out the car keys. "This one is better."

Davi stared at the keys and only got angrier. Her face felt hot and she snorted out her nose.

"I don't want your car. I want my car."

"Too bad, Davida. Your car fucking died. Jesus Christ himself couldn't have resurrected it." Del laughed and dangled the keys again. "Just take it. You earned it."

"No."

"Well, I ain't bringing that other hunk of shit out here. It's already been crushed. So use this one or don't. I couldn't fucking care less." Del dropped the keys on the deck railing.

"How am I gonna explain a brand-new car?" Davi yelled. "You don't think that big Sheriff is going to notice?"

"So what if he does? Has he called you yet, even though you missed a ten-o'clock appointment? No. And he ain't gonna say shit about a car."

"And I guess you're responsible for all that too?" Davi screamed. Blinds began to rattle around the trailer park as the other residents became interested.

"Maybe. What do you care? He ain't gonna bother you no more, and you got a fucking car, so what's the problem?"

"I just want you to leave me alone. I don't know what you think I'm going to do, but trust me, it won't have anything to do with you and whatever it is that you do," Davi said, trying to calm her voice.

Del nodded. "I get that, but maybe I just want to help you."

Davi shook her head. "Don't insult my intelligence. You want me to do something. You made me an accessory to murder. That wasn't even necessary, but you went the extra mile. You don't just want to help me."

"I told you, I want you to work for me."

"Doing what? Cooking meth? Prostitution? Theft? Work at a strip club?" Davi shook her head. "I know what you do, and I don't want any part of it."

"I haven't figured it out yet, but it won't be illegal."

"Everything that you do is illegal. Even if what you ask me to do isn't illegal, it's still going to be illegal."

Del laughed. "You got me there. How about we compromise? I'll find you a job that ain't got nothing to do with me."

"Why?"

"I want you and whatever it is that you do, right where I can fucking see you," Del replied.

"So, keep your friends close and your enemies closer?"

Del's grin faded. "You don't want me for either, Davida," she said darkly. "Take the car. Go get your kid. Go to work. We'll talk later."

Del walked away and got into Jimmy's big truck. She rolled the window down. "Oh, there's groceries in the back. Might wanna get them in the fridge and freezer."

Davi closed her eyes and tried to calm herself. She wasn't successful. When she opened them, Del was smiling and waving.

Davi flipped her off.

Del returned the gesture but maintained her smile as the truck backed out of the drive.

When Davi looked inside the Civic, she was shocked to find several bags of groceries. Canned goods, milk, meats to freeze, produce, kid food, lunch meat, bread, and snacks—food enough to last them a month, easy. The food enraged her further, but Davi wasn't wasteful or too proud to take it. She put it away as fast as she could and kept mental track of the amount that she was going to pay back to Delilah Monroe if she ever saw her again. Davi knew without a doubt she would see her again.

When she picked up Alex, he was so excited about the new car that he could barely sit still.

"Where'd you get it? It's so cool!" he yelled as he used the switch to roll the windows up and down. "Holy crap, Mom, it's got a real radio!"

Davi was ashamed that a functioning radio and working power windows were all it took to impress her son. "Don't break that window. It's only ours for a little while."

"What? No! We need to keep it. It sounds so much quieter than the old car. Is it really running?"

She almost laughed at that. The old car had been loud. The muffler was barely hanging on and she knew there was a hole in the exhaust somewhere. This car ran smooth and easy. It was unsettling to her, too.

"It's fine. Just sit down and don't mess it up."

"Oh, I won't!" he said. "I love our new car!"

When they got home, she had no choice but to call off her shift at the restaurant. The Friday manager was a hateful old lady. She yelled and threatened Davi, but Davi stayed calm. She had despair in the pit of her stomach when she hung up and thought about being short on her rent. Maybe it was good they had the car. They could live in it for a while.

"Oh my gosh, MOM," Alex screamed. "How did we get Twinkies? Did you win the lottery?"

Alex ripped open the box and shoved two of the greasy yellow snack cakes in his mouth before she could stop him. "That's enough of that!" Davi grabbed the box and put them in the upper cabinet that Alex couldn't get to.

She was an accessory to murder, indebted to a criminal, and probably unemployed. Today had most definitely not been her lucky day.

CHAPTER 9

WHEN DAVI WOKE up the next morning, Alex was already awake and happily eating a bowl of Fruit Loops as he watched cartoons. He grinned at her, and she sat down on the couch next to him.

"Mom, we got real Fruit Loops. Not the kind in the bag," he said around a mouthful of cereal.

"Don't talk with your mouth full," Davi said. What was she doing wrong as a parent and an adult that her kid got that excited about name brand cereal? She remembered how that felt as a kid, to never have the name brand of anything, and what a feeling of triumph it had been to finally get Fruity Pebbles or have a pair of Levi jeans, not the Faded Glory brand from Walmart. She felt like she was failing as a mother.

Alex was so happy about his Fruit Loops that he ignored

her admonishment and went right back to enjoying his cereal and cartoons without comment. He giggled and slurped the sugar-scummed milk as he watched Jerry the mouse hit Tom the cat with a 2x4.

Davi wished that somebody would hit her in the face with a 2x4. Maybe that would be an excuse to get out of work in a few hours. The problem was, based on recent events, she was fairly certain the lumber would fare worse than her face. She needed the money, so calling out sick was not an option, but she still had nobody to watch Alex. Brian hadn't answered at all yesterday. Davi was beginning to be resigned to unemployment. She thought maybe it was just easier to quit and find a new job. She'd do it if she had any money at all saved, but she was broke, not so much as a penny in savings, and the rent was due in a week.

Davi watched Alex as he happily shoved spoonfuls of Fruit Loops in his mouth. He deserved better than this, better than this constant scraping and fighting for a few dollars to buy generic mac and cheese and pay rent on a shitty trailer. She could move back in with her mom. She'd still be screwed though, because just like the trailer park slumlord demanded rent on the first, her mom would expect a share of the bills, so she wouldn't be much better off. She'd still owe money, and she would have to listen to her mom's constant bitching. Davi would also have to quit school. Her school schedule created conflicts that her mom wouldn't help her resolve, and especially wouldn't help her resolve if she lived there.

Davi could move in, work, and save until she had enough to get back on her feet. Her mom's rent was cheaper, and a regular day job would help her put back enough to get out on her own again. The problem was, that was exactly what she had done before. She'd had a nice bit of savings when she'd moved out of her mom's place a year ago, but life, kids, medical bills, school, slow weeks at work—they all had a way of chipping away at that nest egg, penny by penny, dollar by dollar, until there wasn't anything left and Davi was right back to where she started from, which was nowhere.

Davi stared at the TV screen without really watching it and felt that far away sense of hopelessness, as if she were adrift on a raft in the ocean with no ability to help herself. That wasn't true; she had options, she just hated all of them. Her mood turned darker, contrasting with the silly noises of the cartoon and Alex's laughter. Davi was shaken out of the funk by a loud, authoritative bang on the door. Only one kind of person knocked on a door like that.

She opened the door and found herself staring at the big burly sheriff. He tipped his hat to her, but he looked serious.

"Miss Barker."

Davi swallowed hard and her heart raced. She nodded back. "Sheriff."

"Mind if I come in?"

The warning bells in Davi's head were telling her not to let him in. She had a vague recollection that she shouldn't ever let cops in a house without a warrant. She didn't have anything to hide though, except her truth. He could be trying to trick her into revealing that. She looked him in the eye. He was burly, broad-shouldered, and strong, but he had a gentle look for such a big man, and he spoke in a quiet, respectful voice. His face was young, but it was aged up by the neat beard her wore. His eyes were gentle and sad. She didn't sense any deceit in this man.

"I suppose you can come in," Davi said. She opened the screen door and motioned him inside.

The sheriff nodded, ducked, and had to turn sideways to get through the door. He took off his hat and stood inside the living room. Alex stared at him, open-mouthed.

"Hello, young man," the sheriff said.

Alex kept staring.

"Don't be impolite, Alex," Davi growled.

"Hello," Alex managed. "Did you come to take us to jail?"

"Why would I need to haul you off to jail? You done something?"

Alex shook his head. "No. I sure didn't."

"I called him because you won't clean up your room," Davi said. "You better go clean it or he'll haul you off."

"He won't either," Alex giggled. "That ain't illegal."

"It's illegal not to do what your mom says," the sheriff said. He looked stern. Alex's eyes got wide.

"Is it really?" he asked in a small voice. Davi wanted to laugh at the panicked look on Alex's face, but she was more worried about the sheriff's intent than in the comedy at the moment.

"It's illegal," the sheriff nodded. "So maybe you best go

check and make sure that room is neat. I'll discuss it with your mama."

Alex jumped off the couch and ran back the hallway to his room. He slammed the door closed, and Davi could hear him rummaging around, hopefully cleaning and keeping busy.

"Sorry about the other day. My car broke down," Davi said. It was a ridiculous excuse.

"That happens. Wish you would have called me," he said.

"Yeah, well…" Davi really didn't know what to say so she didn't. She just shrugged.

"Best not to beat around the bush," the sheriff said. "You're in a mess of trouble, Davida. Let me help you get out of it."

Her stomach lurched, and it felt like she'd dropped about a hundred feet in the air. He was right. She was in a mess of trouble. She definitely needed help getting out of it, but she highly doubted the big burly sheriff was going to be the one to do it.

"Look, sheriff, I'm sorry about the other day. Really. But I ain't in any trouble unless that guy comes back to rob me again, and I doubt he does that. Probably long gone. Tweakin' out Hill's Hollow way, like they do," Davi said. She tried to keep her voice calm and even, tried to sound convincing, but to her ears it all came out rushed and higher pitched than her normal voice.

The sheriff looked at her and nodded. "No, I don't reckon you're in any danger from that feller at all." He stared at her a beat before he continued. "It ain't like Del to leave no bodies around to find."

Davi stared back at him, afraid if she looked away it would be an admission of guilt. She wanted to ask him who Del was, but his face, although still calm and kind looking, read as if he knew that she knew exactly who Del was, and he was daring her to deny it.

"Delilah Monroe is no friend to count on," he said quietly. There wasn't any malice or anger in his voice. It was sad. "It's in your best interest to steer clear of her."

"Sheriff, you got any real questions for me?" Davi asked. Maybe he was going to ask her for help. She didn't know. Davi certainly didn't think she could help him, and she knew without a doubt if she admitted that she knew Delilah Monroe, it would open up a river of shit she wouldn't be able to slog her way out of.

"I got all kinds of questions for you, Davida, but I doubt you'll answer 'em."

"Then what did you come out here for?" Davi asked.

He sighed and rubbed his beard. "I wanted to get the measure of you, and I hoped maybe she hadn't sunk too far in yet, but I can see now she has."

"Sheriff, I don't kno—"

He held up his hand and stood up from the couch. He looked massive, like a bear. The hand he held up looked like it could palm Davi's head. "Don't lie. Don't say nothing. I know you're scared. You should be. Just know I ain't going away, and if you want my help, all you gotta do is call."

"I don't need any help. I'll be just fine. All I want to do is mind my own business," Davi said.

The sheriff nodded as he exited the trailer and walked down the rickety wood steps to his cruiser. He settled his hat on his head. "I know. But it's too late for that now," he said. "You got my number, Miss Barker." He tipped his hat to her one last time, then climbed into his car and drove off.

CHAPTER 10

Davi had never considered herself very good at sweet-talk or contrition, but she employed both to get her job back. She called Patty, the only manager Davi thought she would have any luck with, and through almost an hour of apologies and explanations of life circumstances, Davi somehow managed to convince Patty to let her on that evening's schedule. She couldn't mess this up. Davi knew she had to make it through the night, then would have to go and talk to her mom, who would be back from the gambling trip in the morning, and who might be more inclined to help Davi if her and her boyfriend came home with a few dollars from Keno. Nothing about the next twenty-four hours was likely to be pleasant, but Davi was used to that.

Davi got ready for her shift and tried not to think too

hard about the poor choice she was about to make. All the sweet talk and contrition had only solved one problem, which was getting her job back. What to do with Alex for the night was still an issue. She couldn't leave him at home by himself. With nobody to babysit, she only had one option and that was to take him with her, only, she couldn't bring him in the restaurant. It was Saturday night, their busiest, and there wouldn't be any available tables, not to mention she was on thin ice anyway and couldn't afford to cause any distractions or problems for Patty or any of the other managers.

Her only choice—although she detested it—was to keep him in the car. She hated it. She hated it with every fiber of her being, but she couldn't see any other option. She needed the money, and this was her shot at it. So, armed with coloring books, Legos, two boxes of Twinkies, a bag of Doritos, and his Star Wars blanket, Alex came to work with her.

"I'm going to check on you every fifteen minutes," Davi said as she tied her apron. "I think we'll only be here a couple of hours. Listen to me, Alex." She snapped her fingers at him and furrowed her brow into her most serious face. "You do not get out of the car. You hear me?"

He nodded. "Yes, Mom."

"Okay. Good. If there is an emergency, run right to that door and come in." Davi pointed to the To-Go entrance. She bent down and kissed his head. Alex settled in and played with his Legos. Davi shut the car door and looked at him one last time. He was happily playing and munching chips. As Davi walked away, she had a panicky feeling in her gut. She knew she wasn't doing the right thing. Good mothers didn't leave kids in cars, even when it wasn't hot or freezing cold, Davi knew this wasn't what good mothers did, but, good mothers also didn't live in cars and let their kid starve, so she sucked back that feeling of regret and concentrated on getting her shift done as quickly as possible.

Davi got two tables right out of the gate, and she got them sorted efficiently. She finished putting in their orders, then popped outside to check Alex. He was fine. He was still singing and playing. Davi handed him a soda and asked him if he had to pee. He shook his head no as he slurped his root beer, a rare treat for him, and continued on with his games.

The first check made her feel a little better. He was fine and entertained. Davi was able to check on him two more times before getting three tables all at once. She let the moron hostess have a piece of her mind, but kept the tables, as they were money, and concentrated on getting drinks and taking orders. She did it well, considering she had three groups to attend to, but it did take her a while to get things settled down. Davi wasn't able to make her fifteen-minute checks, and a little over a half hour passed before she could run out to the car and check him.

When she got there, her stomach dropped, and her heart stopped. Alex wasn't in the car.

The Legos were there, and his coloring book was open to

a half-finished picture of Darth Vader, the black crayon abandoned in the seam of the book, but Alex was not there.

Davi couldn't think. She couldn't breathe. She doubled over and tried to catch her breath. Her mind whirled. Alex understood the orders. He wouldn't have gotten out of the car.

Or would he? Sometimes he didn't listen, and she thought maybe he had sucked back the soda so fast that he needed to pee. Davi ran inside through the To-Go door and straight into the men's restroom without knocking. There was only one man in there, standing at the urinal, and he jumped when she burst through the door and yelled, "Alex?"

But Alex wasn't in there. Not in either of the disgusting stalls, which she slammed open and searched, screaming for him.

"Jesus, lady, ain't nobody else in here," the man yelled as he put his dick away and looked offended.

"A little boy. Did you see a little boy in here?" She stopped herself just short of grabbing the man by the shirtfront and shaking him.

"No. There wasn't nobody in here when I come in," the man said.

Davi flexed her hands and controlled them. She held them out in front of her as she felt the surge of energy through her body. The man didn't seem like he was lying, but could she take that chance? Davi looked down at his hand, then back up at his face. He stared at her stupidly and she screamed. She grabbed his hand.

He looked confused for a second as he stared at their hands. He tried to pull away, but when Davi held his hand tight, he jerked harder. She didn't let go, and when she squeezed, he yelled and fell to his knees.

"Did you see a little boy in here?" she asked, half sobbing.

The man threw up; the vomit splashed all over the urinal and down the wall.

"No!" he screamed.

Davi squeezed a little more and he yelled again. "I-I swear. No little boys. I like old ladies. Grannies. I got a whole collection of 'em. Sometimes I like to sit outside the nursing home and I—"

"Alright. Jesus. Shut up," Davi said as she let go of his hand.

He sank to the floor, vomited once again, then he cried.

Davi had no time for him any longer as he was of no help. She stormed out of the restroom. She found Lacey, the girl on To-Go.

"You see my kid come in here?"

Lacey shook her head. "No. Why would he come in here?"

Davi didn't answer. Her ears perked up as she heard a familiar giggle. Davi stalked over to table sixteen, the big round corner booth. Her face was hot, and she was mad, but she also felt the prickly panic sensation course through her as she stared at her kid sitting in the booth enjoying a chocolate milkshake. The fat, pasty neighbor, Jerry, sat next to him, and sitting across from them both was Delilah Monroe.

"Alex." Davi was barely able to croak out his name. "Get up from there immediately."

"Mom, I got a milkshake, and Jerry and me are gonna get wings." Alex poked his straw around in the ice cream and seemed unworried.

"I said, get up," Davi barked. She didn't look at Alex. She maintained eye contact with Del.

"Take it easy there, Davida," Del said in a too- pleasant tone.

"You don't need to say a word," Davi spat. "Alex, get up and let's go."

"Sit down, Davida," Del said. "The kid is just having a milkshake."

Alex still refused to get up. "No. I'm hungry."

Jerry looked up at Davi. He tried to smile, but he looked nervous. "Sorry, Davi, but he's fine. Honest."

Davi ignored Jerry and addressed Del. "You took my child."

"You left your child in a car for the night," Del said evenly.

"That's no concern of yours," Davi said. "You kidnapped him."

"And brought him to Applebee's where his mama was and fed him ice cream. Call the fucking FBI," Del said. "Or maybe I should call somebody? How about CPS? They'd be interested to know somebody left a little boy in a car while they waited tables all night."

Davi slammed her hand down on the table. Her palm

cracked and dented the Formica in a perfect shape of her hand. She felt the anger and energy surge through her.

Del seemed to feel it too. She growled long and low as she gripped the side of the table, crushing the plastic and fake wood.

"You want a fight, Davida, you gonna get it. Or, you could sit the fuck down."

"I'm not afraid of you," Davi said. She didn't move.

"I know you ain't. Otherwise, I wouldn't be bothering with you." Del motioned to the space next to Alex. "Sit down."

"Mommy?" Alex said. His voice seemed smaller than normal and he looked up at Davi, worry evident on his little face.

Davi sat down slowly. "Alex. Finish that shake, now." She put her arm around him and pulled him close.

"I found a job for you," Del said.

"I have a job," Davi replied.

"You ain't keepin' it. Not even if you want to."

"You don't know anything."

"I know Old Fat Patty Rotten Crotch ain't gonna let you stay much longer, not after making this ruckus," Del said. "I know a guy. Needs a secretary. Receptionist. Whatever. He'll work with your schedule."

"Convenient," Davi said. "Same office you shot that tweaker in or a different one?"

Del looked non-plussed. "Oh a different one. Guy's on the up and up. He's an accountant."

"On the up and up? I highly doubt that. He works for you."

"He don't. Not at all."

"No."

Del shook her head. "I'm trying to help you, Davi."

"I don't want or need your help," Davi said. "Leave me alone."

Del smiled and leaned back against the plastic booth seat. "You might not want it, but you need it. You won't be able to get work in this town if I say that's so."

"I doubt that," Davi said. She stood up and yanked Alex out of the booth.

"I promise you, it's a fact. Old Patty is gonna can you right now," Del said as she nodded toward the back of the restaurant. Patty was watching them with a red face and bitchy expression, her lips pursed and white with anger.

"I'll find another job," Davi said.

"You won't. Not unless I say so."

Davi shook her head. "You're delusional." But was she? Davi had a sinking feeling in her stomach, and she knew this situation was out of control.

"Well, I guess you're gonna test it. Go on ahead. I'll be waiting." Del sat there, smiling smugly.

"Come on Alex," Davi said, never taking her eyes off Del.

Jerry finally broke his silence, and he grabbed Davi's arm. "Listen, Davi, please—"

Davi looked down at his hand on her forearm She furrowed her brow, confused, his grip was cold and strong.

She grabbed Jerry's forearm with her other hand and squeezed as she focused her energy and felt it travel down her hand and into him.

Jerry looked at his arm and his face contorted in pain. Welts and burns began to form on his face. A huge cold sore burst out on his lip. The flesh on his arm where Davi held him began to turn dark—black and mottled green, like it was rotting, and there was a sickly-sweet smell in the air.

Jerry looked over at Del and cried, "Del?"

Del didn't answer, but she growled, a low rumble, and squeezed the table until it cracked and splintered.

Alex began to cry. "Mommy?"

His voice snapped Davi out of the strange angry trance that she was in, and she let go of Jerry's arm. He collapsed back against the booth seat, sobbing as he held his ruined arm. The arm was black and rotten from elbow to wrist.

Davi wanted to vomit. Not from the putrid smell of rotting flesh that hung heavy in the air but from the realization that she caused it.

"Stay away from us," she said, pointing a shaking finger at Del.

"Ain't no way that's happening now, Davida," Del growled. "But go on and get out of here now. I'll be in touch."

Davi didn't say anything. She pulled Alex away from the table, tossed her apron to Patty on her way out, and drove home. She put the terrified Alex to bed. Once he was in bed, Davi sat on the couch and stared at her hands. She had made Jerry rot. She made Brian and the man in the restroom confess their darkest secrets, and she had no idea how she had done it. Panic settled into her chest, a vise grip on her heart. She breathed in deep to help it go away, but that didn't work, and her mind whirled and throbbed as she put her face in her hands and cried.

CHAPTER 11

ON MONDAY MORNING, Davi dropped Alex off at school, then headed out to find a job. No amount of sweet talk on her part was going to help her at the restaurant. Davi had two nasty voicemails from Fat Patty on Sunday demanding Davi turn in her extra work shirts immediately. There were other restaurants in town. There was a Dairy Queen, but it was mostly staffed by pimple-pocked teens and didn't pay enough to deal with the high school drama and smell of sour ice cream mix. She couldn't go to the Golden Corral either. The hours wouldn't fit with school, and the ten percent tips from large families of fat white trash and old geezers on a fixed income wouldn't pay her rent.

The IGA was an option, so she started there. She loathed Skippy Bowman, the manager of the IGA. He was in his late forties, had never been seen with a woman, wore those oversized wire rimmed glasses favored by low income religious types and child molesters, and he stared at her tits. Davi had an interview at the grocery store before, and Skippy had never looked her in the eye at all. He stared at her chest and licked his chapped lips compulsively as he grilled her about her customer service skills and ability to count back change. In the end, she had taken the waitress job because when tips were good, it paid well. The IGA was barely above minimum wage, and if somebody was going to ogle her breasts, Davi decided she'd like to be tipped well for it.

She showed up at the beginning of the application window, which started at 9 am, and waited patiently for Skippy to call her back to his office. Nobody else was there to apply, but Davi had to wait forty-five minutes for Skippy to emerge. He held a clipboard and looked around nervously, avoiding Davi to the point of ridiculousness. He searched all around the area and huffed loudly, quite obviously desperate to find anyone else but her.

Davi shook her head and sighed, then stood up and plastered a fake smile on her face. She was adept at it. "Hey, Ski-Mr. Bowman. I came about the open cashier position."

Skippy jumped when she spoke to him, and he was pasty and sweaty. He avoided looking at her all together. When his eyes didn't jump right to her tits, Davi knew she wasn't getting a job.

"Oh umm… well we've already hired for that job," Skippy said. He wiped his sweaty palms on his thick polyester slacks, then adjusted his clip-on tie.

"Really? The sign is still in the store window," Davi said as she pointed at the Help Wanted sign plastered on the glass next to the big sale add for canned corn.

"Yes. I-I just filled it last night. Didn't have a chance yet to pull down the sign," he mumbled.

"That's a shame. I really need a job, sir. You got any other openings? I'll do anything. Clean, stock shelves, work in the deli." Davi pointed to the ancient old lady frying chicken for the lunch rush.

"No. As I said, we don't have no openings," Skippy huffed. He looked around the store as if he expected somebody to jump out and scare him. "If you'll excuse me, I have paper-work to do."

Davi nodded and tried to smile. She offered him the application she filled out, but he stared at it. "Well, you mind taking my application, sir? It's got my phone number on it, so if something comes up, you'll call me?"

He looked at the paper, then at her and back at the paper. "I'm sure we have it on file, umm… Daveena."

"It's Davida, sir. Davida Barker." She stepped closer and pushed the application at him. He edged back from her like she was trying to hand him a rattlesnake.

"Yes, Davida, well I have your information." He still didn't take it. Davi knew he never would.

"Okay, sir. Thanks for your time."

Skippy nodded at her then sprinted back inside the office.

Davi was met with the same result no matter where she

applied that morning. The CVS Pharmacy, the ACE Hardware store, the Duke Gas Station, even the old lady at the Dairy Queen turned her away.

"I gotta be better than the kids you hire," Davi said.

"Oh for sure, honey," the old woman said around her cigarette, "but I ain't gonna cross a Nolan."

"What's that mean?" Davi asked, even though she already knew the answer.

"You already know," the old woman said as she shrugged and closed the order window.

Delilah Monroe was as good as her word. There wasn't a place that was going to hire her. She sat in her car and cried angry tears. She'd like to see if she could rot Delilah Monroe fully. If she'd been able to do it to Jerry's arm, she was sure she could do it to Del with enough time and concentration. She was imagining the satisfying black skin and smell when someone knocked on her car window. She jumped, then her face flushed hot and she narrowed her eyes in rage.

"Roll it down and don't get out of the car," Del said calmly.

Davi considered gunning the Civic, but she'd have to back up, and one of the big black pickups had whipped in to block her escape. She rolled down the window and scowled. "You can fuck right off."

"You ain't ready to listen to reason?"

"I won't bother you. I won't interfere with you at all," Davi said.

"Well now, you might say that, Davida, but what if somebody tries to change your mind?"

"Like who? I don't know anybody."

Del shrugged. "Lots of people. Somebody is gonna talk about what you can do."

"What do you plan to do? Kill me?" Davi asked.

"I ain't sure I could," Del said. "But I doubt it comes to that. I don't want to see anybody get hurt."

"Then leave me alone."

"If you don't want nobody to get hurt, and you wanna make a living for your kid, all you gotta do is let me help."

"You made sure I can't get any other jobs," Davi said.

"I sure did," Del nodded. "I might be a lot of things, Davi, but a liar ain't one of them."

"Nice you have standards. Too bad murder isn't on that list."

"Come on. Like you care about that idiot. He fucking shot you and would do it again if he thought he could get ten bucks for crank."

"Well he can't now," Davi said. Del was right. Davi wasn't particularly sad about the man, but she hadn't wanted to see anyone shot to death. She'd blocked that part out for the most part, and even more so, she shoved deep down inside the fact that she really didn't care.

"Nope. He sure can't. And nobody gives a shit," Del said. She pulled a slip of paper out of her pocket. "Tomorrow. Nine in the morning. After you drop the kid off. Go by that office. Guy's name is Gayle. He's expecting you."

"And what if I don't?" Davi asked.

"You're smarter than that Davida," Del said as she handed her the paper.

Davi took the slip and tossed it on the seat beside her. "Are you threatening me?"

"No," Del said. She didn't smile and she didn't look away. Davi understood.

"If you go near him, I'll kill you," Davi said.

Del nodded. "I don't hurt little boys."

Davi scoffed. "I doubt you have any limits."

"Believe what you want," Del said. She stuffed her hands in the pockets of her jeans. "Just show up tomorrow at nine."

Davi didn't say anything. Del stared at her a beat, rolled her eyes, then walked away. Davi looked at the scrap of paper. The address written on it was familiar to her. It was a little office next to the hardware store. She almost threw the slip out the window, but the reality of her situation was that she had no job and she wasn't going to get another one unless Del arranged it. She was afraid of the threat, but not for Alex. Delilah Monroe was a murderer. Davi had witnessed her kill, but she sensed that Del was telling the truth when she said she wouldn't hurt Alex. That confused her and went against good sense, but Davi knew it to be true. Just because she didn't believe that Del would hurt Alex didn't mean she thought Del wouldn't hurt Davi's mom, or somebody else, and she wouldn't put it past Del to do something malicious that might separate her and Alex. Anybody who had enough clout to keep her from getting a job certainly had enough pull to get CPS involved in Davi's life.

The next morning, after she dropped Alex off at school, she hesitated for a minute as she sat parked across the street from the little office. She banged her fists on the steering wheel and screamed, but it was impotent rage, because she knew she was going to get out of the car and go inside.

The office was small and sparsely outfitted. The outer room was only big enough for a small desk and a couple of cheap metal office chairs. They were shiny and brand-new. Davi doubted any ass had ever sat in them. The desk was cheap MDF board, but it was pristine and unblemished. The computer and telephone system were new too, and Davi could smell the plastic smell she associated with new electronics.

Gayle McNabb came out of a back office and shook her hand. She didn't know Gayle and had never seen him around town. It wasn't like she knew everyone in town but working at the restaurant meant that she knew a good portion of the townsfolk that could afford an office, and oddly, she had never encountered Gayle. His cheap beige dress shirt and brown polyester slacks were the blandest outfit Davi had ever seen, and Gayle's face itself was just a slightly doughy extension of that cheap dress shirt. The coloring was so similar Davi had to look twice to see where the shirt ended and the man's face began. Gayle had the look of a person who was transparent and not real, like a copy of a copy.

"Your job is to answer the phone and watch the door,"

THE HARD TRUTH | 85

Gayle said in a monotone voice. His eyes looked past her even though he looked right at her.

"You just need me to answer phones?" Davi asked.

"And file things when there's things to file," Gayle said.

"Okay, umm… what are the hours?" Davi hoped he said hours at the times she had class.

"Nine in the morning until two in the afternoon on days you don't have classes," Gayle replied.

"How do you know about my classes?" Davi asked.

"I know," Gayle said. He stared at her and didn't elaborate.

So the job was perfect hours for her school schedule and to make sure she could pick up Alex. She wasn't shocked, more annoyed by the acquiescence.

"It's twenty dollars an hour," Gayle said. "You can start tomorrow."

He showed her a small kitchenette area with a tiny refrigerator and a microwave. His office was Spartan. There were no personal effects, no office art hung on the walls, and his furniture was new too.

Davi doubted the office had existed before a few days ago. It was fishy, all of it, but Delilah Monroe was involved so fishy was the least of Davi's concerns. Much stronger words were likely applicable.

"Alright, Mr. McNabb. I guess I'll see you tomorrow morning."

He nodded at her and neither smiled nor frowned. Davi decided his face was incapable of emotion at all.

She thought for a second about using whatever power she had, make him tell the truth, but she didn't really know if she could control it, and that scared her. Besides, she already knew the truth, which was that while Gayle McNabb might have an office and sign her paychecks, she worked for Delilah Monroe whether she liked it or not. She didn't like it, not one little bit.

CHAPTER 12

DAVI SCOWLED as Alex slammed the Civic door and bounded across the yard to Jerry's trailer.

"Alex, get back here!" she yelled. She slammed her own door closed and hoisted the bag in her left arm.

"I'm just going to talk to Jerry a minute."

"Alex, I mean right—"

Davi stopped as Jerry came out of his trailer. He looked at her fearfully and held a hand up in a half-hearted wave. His good hand. The other one hung limply at his side. His forearm where Davi touched him was covered in a long sleeve t-shirt. Wet spots seeped through the fabric of the t-shirt. Jerry got closer, and when he was within about ten feet of her, Davi gagged. He smelled strongly of rotten hamburger meat. He kept the distance between them.

"Hey Jerry," Alex said. He wrinkled his nose. "Smells like garbage."

"Alex, go inside right now," Davi said.

"But Mom—"

"Right now!"

Her tone was sufficiently angry that Alex jumped to attention, then slumped into a pout and trudged back across the sparse trailer park grass and into the trailer.

"It's okay Davi. I won't hurt him," Jerry said. "I won't hurt you either."

"Like you could," Davi said. "Stay away from us."

"Del won't allow it," Jerry said.

"I won't allow you to creep around me or my kid. I can't do anything about your boss right now, but I can sure as hell deal with you." Davi nodded toward his rotten arm.

"Do you even know what you can do?" he asked.

"I know I messed you up," Davi said. "And if you don't leave us alone, I'll finish it."

"I'm not your enemy," he said.

"You sure as hell aren't my friend," Davi spat.

"I could be. I want to be," Jerry said. "I'm not going to lie to you. Dealing with Del ain't always smart, but now you got no choice. Just stay calm. I'll help you, and Del ain't... well, she ain't bad all the time."

"She's a fucking drug dealer. I saw her kill a man," Davi said.

"Yeah. She is and she surely did," Jerry agreed. "But she won't hurt Alex."

"I don't believe that," Davi said. She watched Jerry's face as he measured her for a few seconds. He looked thoughtful and sad.

"Yes you do," he said. "I won't lie to you and tell you that Del won't look out for herself, 'cause she will. That's what she does. But I've known her all her life, and I know she won't hurt your kid."

"Why should I believe a family full of criminals?" Davi asked. She didn't even know why she was asking or trying to disagree with him at this point. All her life, she had avoided the traps of the county. She didn't do drugs. She wasn't popular or rich. She didn't run with the hoodly girls or date the greasy boys. Davi was the middle. The mediocre. The girl you barely noticed. She worked hard because she had to. She wasn't gifted or fortunate enough to have family money to get her going in life. All she had was hard work and the drive to get out. The kid had thrown a monkey wrench into her plan, but she still kept going, kept moving toward the goal of getting clear of the County. Her powers and new affiliation with Delilah Monroe threatened to upset all that, to hold her back, not propel her forward, and that was what she was afraid of, not of physical violence but of stalling out.

"I don't know," Jerry said, shrugging his shoulders, "I guess I wouldn't believe us entirely either. You ain't exactly helpless, though. I ain't holding a grudge, so that ought to count for something." He motioned to his ruined, stinking arm.

He was right. Or he was an excellent liar. Davi looked at

his disgusting arm and shivered. She didn't want to admit that she had no idea how she had done it to him. He was correct, she wasn't defenseless.

"Can't you just leave us alone? Wouldn't that be better for you?"

Jerry nodded. "Likely so," he agreed. "But that ain't how Del is going to play it."

"We could run."

"The surest way to get Del to chase you is to run," Jerry said. "You'd never get away from her, believe me. Best thing for you to do is to relax. A door can't stay closed forever."

Davi laughed at him. "It sure can. If nobody ever opens it."

Jerry nodded. "Exactly."

CHAPTER 13

"DAVIDA, I HAVE FILES," Gayle said. His voice was flat and monotone. Davi thought it would be a good idea to record Gayle's flat voice and play it on a loop when she had trouble falling asleep.

She got up from her desk and picked up the files he deposited in the tray that hung on his door. The manila folders were labeled with red strip file folder labels. That meant it was Tuesday. Gayle used red labels on Tuesdays, blue on Wednesdays, and purple on Thursdays. He generated exactly ten folders each day. Inside each was a single invoice. They were always to the same ten companies. Davi snooped around and figured out that the companies were made up. They weren't shell companies or anything like that, they were fictitious.

It took Davi exactly three minutes to file the ten folders.

In an eight-hour work day, that was the only actual work that she did. The rest of the time, she did homework. She had never been so caught up on all her classwork. Study sessions had always been stolen moments between shifts or late-night efforts after Alex was in bed. Now she was ahead in almost every class, and her grades had noticeably improved. Her biology professor commented on it when she picked up a quiz.

"Be careful, Barker," he told her as he handed her the paper. "You might start to expect success from yourself if you keep that up."

She hadn't answered him and had barely kept herself from rolling her eyes. He was an asshole, but it was Del she hated. Del was the architect of Davi's recent academic success, and it enraged her. No matter what she did, she couldn't seem to stop racking up debts to Delilah Monroe.

Davi hadn't seen Del since the day she handed her the address to Gayle's office. She knew Del was watching though. Davi saw the suspiciously clean fleet of black pick-ups cruise by through the big plate glass windows at the office. She always heard them before she saw them; the big Cummins diesel engines announced their presence. Del's pack cruised by, slow, three times a day—just after she got to work, after lunch, and right before she left for the day. She also noticed them parked in the faculty lot at the community college. Seeing them pissed her off, but nobody ever approached her, so she swallowed her hatred of them and decided to bide her time.

What she was hoping for, she didn't know. Jerry had been right about doors not staying closed, but who was going to open the door? She wanted to be the one to open it. Every time she saw one of Del's boys in those big black trucks, she wanted to blast the door open herself.

An opportunity to do so hadn't presented itself thus far, so Davi tempered her anger with the pursuit of knowledge. With her classwork under control, she focused on a different education—figuring out her powers.

She started on the Internet. She felt like an idiot, typing *powers* in a search engine, but she didn't know where else to start. As it turned out, Googling was useless. She found nothing she deemed trustworthy or helpful. She wondered if a pastor or priest could help her, but the idea of asking them seemed ridiculous. She wasn't a churchgoer, and the only pastor she knew was the one from her mom's old church. Davi's mom went through a Pentecostal phase and the pastor that jumped around and jibber-jabbered was the only version of a pastor that Davi knew. Her mom had given up the religion after a few months—it had been a hardship to go to that much church—so Davi didn't have much experience with the Lord. She didn't care much about that but having a reliable source of information on the subject of magic might have been beneficial. She couldn't imagine talking to the Pentecostal minister about forcing people to confess terrible secrets and having the ability to rot a man's arm would go well for her, so she remained unenlightened. Davi decided the only thing to do was to do what she had done all her life —wing it.

Davi shoved the filing cabinet drawer closed. She walked into Gayle's office. Gayle stared blankly at his computer monitor. He didn't type or move his mouse, and he didn't acknowledge her at all. Davi cleared her throat.

"So, Gayle. I finished the filing."

Gayle didn't move or look at her. "Yes. Good."

"Is there anything else you want me to work on?"

"I would like you to file the documents," he said in his monotone voice.

"Uh, yeah. I know. I did that already. Do you have anything else? Any other work?"

Gayle's head turned, and he moved his mouth like a gold-fish, like he was trying to form words but couldn't. His eyes focused on Davi and he twitched. "No. Your job is to file the files and answer the telephone."

"I can do other things too," Davi said as she came close to the desk. "I'm good with spreadsheets, basic accounting, website design, you know, lots of stuff that can help."

Gayle's head continued to swivel as she moved to his left. His neck was almost at an unnatural angle, the skin stretched too much, his chin too far past center. "No. Your job is to file the files and answer the telephone." Gayle repeated the information, then twitched. He stood up and looked at her.

Davi didn't back down. She came closer.

"Who are you?" she asked. "What are you?"

"Your job is to file the files and answer the tele—"

Gayle didn't finish. Davi grasped his forearm and concentrated. She felt the heat and energy travel between them, and she squeezed. Unlike everyone else, Gayle didn't cry out, he didn't even look down at his arm. He collapsed in a heap, like somebody dropped a gunny sack of potatoes.

Davi's heart pounded. Had she killed him? Gayle didn't move. He didn't look like he was breathing but she couldn't tell. Davi didn't think she could kill anyone and hadn't had that effect on anyone before, but really didn't know the extent of her power. Now here she was, faced with a body in the middle of the day.

Davi knelt down and rolled Gayle over on his back. She reached two fingers toward his neck to check his pulse but jumped back when she saw his mouth moving in that gold-fish way, forming puckering o's. His wide-open eyes stared blankly at the ceiling.

"You didn't kill him."

Davi jumped again at the voice. A tall, brown-haired woman leaned in the doorway. She pulled her hair back into a low loose ponytail and yawned. "It's okay. Look." The woman motioned to Gayle.

Gayle's mouth opened faster, and he began to hiccup. Davi thought that was worse than the fish mouth.

"What did I do?" Davi asked.

"Drove the spirit out of him. It'll come back though. It's tethered to him. Just give it a minute. Leave him alone and he'll be back to normal in a bit. Well, normal for him, I guess. Come out here with me." The woman held her hand out to

Davi and smiled. Davi hesitated. "You don't understand any of it, do you?" the woman asked.

Davi shook her head. She thought she understood, but she didn't, and now she was completely unsettled and in over her head. "I sure don't."

The woman nodded. She beckoned. "I'm here to help. Come with me and we'll figure you out."

This was the second woman to ask Davi to come with her for help. Davi stood still.

"No offense, but I'm getting really tired of everyone telling me to come with them for help. That's how I got in this mess to start with, so you got something to tell me, just go on and tell me," Davi said.

"Here is where you want to talk?" The woman motioned around the room. "You're sure?"

Davi narrowed her eyes. She understood what the woman was implying. Del most certainly had the office bugged, but this place she knew. This woman, she didn't.

"Yeah. I'm sure. You don't care if she knows you're here and talking to me, otherwise you wouldn't have come. Her, I know. You, I don't, so get on with it or leave me alone." Davi left Gayle twitching on the floor and went back out to her desk. At least the outside door was more accessible should she need it, although, she thought as she flexed her fist and let the energy surge, she wasn't defenseless. Davi sat at her desk and waited.

"Do you know what you are?" the woman asked as she sat down in one of the desk chairs opposite Davi. She relaxed in the chair and as she moved, Davi caught a whiff of something earthy and herbal. It wafted from the woman's long curly hair as she moved. It was a comforting smell. The woman smoothed out her long, Boho-chic skirt then crossed her legs and leaned back in the chair.

"A woman," Davi said.

"Oh you're more than that," the woman said.

"Okay, so what am I then?" Davi felt weird. Small. Like the world was throbbing all around her. The energy prickled her skin.

"You're more," the woman said. "More than a man, more than a woman. You're another level of being. I don't know that we have a word for it."

"That's not really much help, lady," Davi said. She already knew all of that. She couldn't be harmed. She could make people tell things. She could rot flesh, and, apparently, she could make people pass out. None of those things were normal, and she didn't need this woman to explain that part.

"No, I suppose it isn't," the woman said. "You think you know what it is you can do?"

"Not die," Davi said, "And I can make people... tell things."

The woman laughed. "Yes. I guess that's one way to say it, but you're missing it."

"What? What am I missing? I've been shot dead twice and I can hurt people and make them tell me secrets. So what is that? Why is that?" Davi yelled. She was getting agitated. Everyone wanted to talk around the thing, but they wouldn't say the thing.

"Truth, Davida. You make them tell the truth," the woman said quietly.

"What do you mean?" Davi asked. "They just told me stuff."

The woman shook her head. "No. They told you what they really are. What they don't want anyone to know and what they don't want to admit, even to themselves."

Davi's brain whirled. Brian. The man in the bathroom. Jerry. Gayle. None of it seemed connected to truth in her mind.

The woman smiled at Davi's analysis and confusion. "Gayle McNabb disappeared three weeks ago. Before he reappeared here as your employer at whatever fake business this is, he managed a convenience store in Cambridge. He liked to gamble, and he liked pussy. He liked them too much and ended up owing Delilah Monroe a great deal of money. That," the woman pointed through the doorway at Gayle, who had begun to sort of spin around on the floor like a turtle trying to flip itself over, "is what used to be Gayle McNabb, but he isn't there any longer. He's a shell, and when you touched him, you made the creature that inhabits that shell leave for a minute."

"That's impossible," Davi said. "Like a demon? That isn't real."

"Davida, you've been shot twice in the chest and still breathe. Doesn't that word, impossible, mean very little to you these days?"

"How do you know about that?" Davi asked. "Who the hell are you?"

"My name is Racheal Graves. Delilah Monroe isn't the only one who can know things in this town, and I'm one of the people who firmly believes that she shouldn't know them at all."

"Look, I'm not interested in getting in anyone's way. I just want to be left alone," Davi said.

"Davi, nobody is going to leave you alone. You're valuable. You're powerful. Somebody is going to want what you've got or they're going to be afraid of it. You can't hide anymore."

"Let me guess... you're neither?" Davi scoffed.

"I'm not afraid of you. I think you're a wonderous creature," Racheal said.

"Creature? I'm a creature?"

Racheal nodded. "Yes. Beings like you don't come along very often. You've transcended humanity."

"You're giving me too much credit. I didn't do shit." Davi stuffed her books in her book bag and prepared to go. The lady was a crackpot. Maybe Davi could make people tell the truth, but that wasn't all she could do. She did that to Brian. He admitted to being gay. Whatever. Nobody cared. But she had ruined Jerry's arm and apparently driven a demon out of old Gayle. She didn't know what all that was.

Racheal regarded her. "You're the next step up from a human. You're powerful, but that doesn't mean you're invincible. You must be afraid of Delilah or you wouldn't be here. She wants to use you."

"Thanks for the tip. I figured that one out on my own," Davi said. "Any more earth-shattering news you wanna tell me?"

"She'll ruin you. It's what she does. I can stop her. With your help."

Davi stood up. "You're gonna go toe-to-toe with her? You're crazy."

"Do you know what she is?" Racheal asked.

"Drug dealer. Crime boss," Davi said.

"Flesh peddler. Oppressor. Murderer. An animal, really," Racheal said. "She's a cancer on this earth and she needs to be cut out. I need your help to do it."

"How am I supposed to help you? Apparently, I don't even know what I am," Davi said.

Racheal nodded. "That's true, but you know enough to know Delilah Monroe is dangerous. People like her... they use people. She'll say she's not going to hurt you. She'll make overtures and try to help you, but you know what all that is?"

Davi shrugged. "I mean, yeah, it's all lies. I'm not an idiot. I just don't have a choice right now."

"Not true, Davi. You do have a choice. You always have one," Racheal said.

"Spoken like somebody who has never had to make a hard choice. Choices are easy when they're easy," Davi said. She was angry now. Tired of everyone talking at her and telling her how things were. Davi knew how things were.

Most of the time you had to choose between two shitty options. She looked at Racheal in her expensive hippie clothes with her condescending looks and words. She felt the energy buzz up in her. She shivered and closed her eyes.

"Breathe, Davi," Racheal said. "You control it. It doesn't control you."

Davi felt a light touch on her arm and she jerked back. Her eyes flew open. Racheal held her hands out, palm up.

"I'm not going to make you do anything you don't want to do. I just don't want to see her get her claws in you. And she will. It's what she does. I'd spare you the pain."

"She can't hurt me," Davi said. "I can't die."

Racheal shook her head. "Physical pain is nothing. She'll take everything you have, and she'll make you wish you could die."

"I gotta go get my kid. Thanks for explaining what I am, I guess."

Racheal stood up and nodded. She pulled a card from her bag and handed it to Davi. "When you decide you've had enough, call me."

Davi took the card and put it in her bag. "I've already had enough. Of everyone."

CHAPTER 14

"WHAT KIND of job is this, Davida?" Davi's mom lit a cigarette and settled back into the porch swing. Alex chased fireflies in the yard.

"Just an office job," Davi said.

"How'd you know about it?" Her mom looked suspicious. Her mom was always suspicious, although why she cared how Davi got the rent money, Davi didn't know. She had never cared much before unless Davi was asking her for it.

"Just... somebody put me on to it."

"Well, Patty told me she had to fire you for fighting," her mom said.

"Patty is full of shit. And what do you care anyways? I never asked you for anything, and you don't gotta babysit now."

"Who said I was mad about babysitting?" Her mom finished the cigarette and lit another.

"Uh... you did. Every single time I ever asked you to babysit." Davi shook her head. "I came to give you the two hundred I owed you from a few months back."

Davi pulled out an envelope and handed it to her mom. Her mother narrowed her eyes and puffed shallow on the smoke as she looked through the envelope.

"Where did you get all this money?"

"Hooking. Jesus, Mom. I got a job. It pays decent." Davi rolled her eyes.

"Nothing in this town that you'd be qualified for pays this decent," her mom said. "What are you doing at this office?"

"Office work. I mean, look, if you're that bothered by where the money come from, give it back." Davi held out her hand.

Her mom didn't give the envelope back. She tucked it under her thigh and swung back on the porch swing. "No, you ain't to be trusted to pay it back."

"Well I just did, didn't I?" Davi huffed. Every conversation went this way. Antagonistic and hateful. She didn't know why she bothered.

"If I ain't babysitting, who is? I know it ain't his good for nothing father."

That was true. Davi hadn't heard from Brian in three weeks. She wasn't broken up about it, but Alex had been asking about him. She'd need to hunt him down sooner or later, she guessed.

"Nobody. Mr. McNabb works around my schedule."

Davi's mom shook her head and pointed a finger at her. "See, that ain't normal. Offices don't work around your schedule."

"This one does," Davi replied. "You ought to be happy. We won't cramp your style anymore."

"Davida, no good will come of this. Are you taking up with that Monroe woman? I've heard stories about her."

Davi rolled her eyes. "No, mom. I work for Gayle McNabb. I don't have anything to do with Delilah Monroe." Davi yelled to Alex. "Hey, kiddo. Let's go. Time for bath and bed."

Alex caught a firefly in his hands and giggled, then let it go.

"Okay Mom. Gran, can I have a cookie for the road?"

"No. You'll spoil your dinner," Davi said. "Give Grandma a hug. We gotta go."

"He can have one if he wants one, Davida." Her mom got up to go inside. Davi stopped her from opening the screen door.

"No. I said no, and I meant no. Why do you always gotta do that?"

Her mom looked at her. "Do what? I can give my grandson a cookie."

"Undermine me. If I say up, you say down."

"You don't know anything about being a parent," Davi's mom said as she shook her head.

"Oh really? Cause I been doing it for seven years now." Davi slammed the door shut. "What's your real problem here?"

"I don't have a problem. You just don't know as much as you think you know," her mom said. She huffed and knocked Davi's hand off the door.

"No. For once, you tell me what the real problem is," Davi said. It was easy really. It didn't even seem like any effort at all as Davi grabbed her mom's forearm and squeezed ever so slightly. She let the energy flow between them and watched her mom wince and hiss in pain. Davi didn't squeeze harder, she let the energy flow a little faster and repeated the question. "What is the problem?"

Her mom's face reddened and contorted in pain as her mouth opened and closed a few times. "I don't know who your real dad was. I married Carl Barker because I could, and he didn't mind you. I regretted both of you the minute it was all done. You been a burden so long I forget what it was like not to hate you."

Davi let go of her mom's arm as if she was the one who'd been burned. Her mom dropped to her knees on the porch and vomited. She sputtered and spit and coughed. Davi backed away.

"We won't bother you again," Davi said.

"Wait... Davi... I-I didn't mean all that," her mom said as she began to sob.

Davi shook her head and held back tears. Alex began to

cry. Davi hugged him close. "Yes you did. And I guess I didn't need to make you tell me."

"Davi... please," her mom yelled from the porch. Davi ignored her and put Alex in the car. Her mom was still crying and vomiting as Davi pulled away from the curb.

CHAPTER 15

DAVI FOCUSED on the drive and not her mom's confession as she drove home. If she were really honest with herself, she would admit that she really wasn't surprised. She had always known all of it, even the part about her dad. She didn't look anything like him, and she didn't look much like her mom either, but it wasn't that. It was a sense of not belonging, of being the odd person out. Her dad never treated her like she wasn't his. In point of fact, he had been kind and gentle. He liked to take Davi to the park and roll down little hills into piles of leaves they made. She loved him and she knew even though she wasn't quite right and wasn't really his, he had loved her too. He died too young and left her mom too broke and that was something her mom couldn't overcome and couldn't forgive. Davi had always known that too—that there was something there, something about Davi that her mom couldn't reconcile. She didn't need the magic truth touch to confirm it. But it was out there now—the truth—and they would all have to learn to deal with it.

Davi heard the sniffles coming from the backseat. That was the second time that Alex had seen her do whatever it was that she was able to do. She hadn't really talked about it with him the first time. Davi held him and gave him extra cuddles. He bounced back quickly. Tonight was different. He had seen her fight with her mom plenty of times, but he had never seen anything physical between them, nor had he ever heard anything so venomous.

"You okay, bud?" Davi asked.

"Is Gran okay?" Alex croaked.

"She's fine. Don't worry on it." Davi pulled into the trailer park and killed the engine.

"Are we ever gonna see her again?" he asked as he slammed the car door closed.

"Oh I imagine so," Davi replied. "You know I fight with grandma pretty much every day." Davi ruffled his hair and hugged him close as they walked up the steps to the trailer porch.

"You hurt her," Alex said.

Davi nodded. "I didn't mean to," she said. That was a lie. She had known exactly what her touch would do to her mom. It felt good to do it.

"She said mean things," Alex said.

"Everybody says mean things, Alex. Grandma didn't mean to be hateful."

Alex looked up at her. "She meant those ones, but she didn't want you to know."

Davi stared at his little face, right into Brian's big blue eyes sitting in the middle of his face. Alex was a million times smarter than either her or Brian. She leaned down and kissed his forehead. "I know bud. I know. But it's okay."

"But it might not be," Alex said as he cried.

"People say mean things. Sometimes to the people they love. When you love someone you try and get past that."

Alex nodded and sniffed. "Yeah. Sometimes. But you still love me, when I say mean stuff?" He hesitated. "And you don't want to hurt me?"

"I will always love you no matter what." Davi hugged him tight. "And I will never, ever, ever hurt you." Alex hugged her back, and Davi held back the sob that threatened to escape, which she knew would scare Alex more. She swallowed the horror that her baby was worried about what she would do and kissed the top of his head. "You hungry? How about some tacos?"

Alex grinned and nodded. "It's Taco Tuesday!"

"Yep. So you bust out the homework, and I'll make the tacos, deal?"

"Deal," he said.

The immediate problem when Davi opened the door was that her trailer already smelled like taco meat. The other issue was that Delilah Monroe was sitting on the sofa, reading a magazine.

"What the fuck are you doing here?" Davi yelled.

"Mom, you said a bad word," Alex said, pointing at Davi, his attention taken from the stranger sitting on the sofa.

"Alex, go to your room. Now."

Alex didn't argue. He went back the hallway immediately.

"Get out." Davi pointed to the door.

Del put the magazine down. "Calm down, Davida."

"You broke into my house. I'm calling the cops," Davi said.

"Your door was open, and we both know you ain't gonna call the law."

"Just because the door wasn't locked doesn't mean you can come in here. Why in the hell can't you leave me alone?" Davi screamed.

"Because we got business," Del said.

Davi looked around. She wanted to find something to throw. Normally there would have been toys, textbooks, cups, all ready to be hurled, but as Davi looked around, she saw there was no clutter. Everything was neat, and the surfaces were all clear and dusted. She narrowed her eyes and turned to Del.

"Did you fucking clean my house?"

"Uh, yeah. I did. You gonna include that in the police report?" Del laughed.

Davi balled her fists up and looked down at the floor.

"You vacuumed?"

"That's part of cleanin', Davida," Del said.

"Just... I... I can't with you," Davi said as she threw her hands up and went over to the sink. The kitchen was spotless and Del had made the Ortega taco kit that Davi had laid out before she left that morning.

"Best feed that kid. Taco meat's all ready," Del said. She picked up the magazine and went back to looking through it.

Davi felt hot, and she thought that if she were able to see herself, she might actually see steam rising from her, like an angry cartoon character in one of Alex's shows.

She called Alex out, fixed a couple of tacos for him, and sat him down at the table to eat. He ate silently and warily as he watched Del.

Davi didn't eat anything. She went for Del.

"So what business do we have that you feel the need to break in here and make tacos? Couldn't you have just come to your fake office?"

"You know, Davida, this don't have to be a chore," Del said.

"Oh it doesn't?" Davi hissed. "It sure seems like it has to be that way. I can't get away from you. Why are you doing this?"

"What if I only want to help you?"

"You and everyone else," Davi said. "You don't want to help me. You want to control me and use me."

"I think you might be useful, that's true," Del said. "I ain't dumb enough to think I can control you."

"Really? Because you made me take a fake job, and your goons keep tabs on me all day."

"It ain't a fake job. Have the paychecks bounced?" Del smiled, a cross between a laugh and smirk.

It infuriated Davi.

"No real business goes on there, and I don't know what Gayle is, but he ain't real either."

"Just cash the checks Davida."

"Mom, I'm done," Alex said in a small voice. He was still staring at Del.

"Put your plate in the sink," Davi said. Alex did it without complaint then stood by Davi.

Alex looked at Del. "The tacos were good. Did you bring any ice cream?"

Del laughed. "No. Sorry. I guess I owe you one," she said.

"Alex, go back to your room. Homework. Don't come out until I come get you."

"Aww… no. Can we go get ice cream?" he whined.

Davi realized that Alex wasn't scared of Del at all. He'd been more scared of her. He looked over at Del as if she could overrule Davi.

"Homework. Now." Davi snapped her finger and pointed back the hall.

"Fine." He gave a little half-stomp, then walked back to his room.

"He drives a hard bargain," Del laughed.

"You don't need to worry anything about him," Davi said. She sat down in the ratty brown chair across from Del. "What the hell is this Delilah? You think this thing ends with us as friends?" She looked hard at Del for a second. "Or anything else? No chance."

"I don't know how it ends for us, but I know how it ends for you if you mess around with Racheal Graves."

It was Davi's turn to laugh. "I wondered when you'd get around to her. I knew you saw that."

"Stay away from her."

"Funny, that's what she advised I do about you."

"She would. She ain't what she pretends to be."

"And you are?"

Del shrugged. "I've never once lied to you."

Davi had to admit that was true. She knew exactly what Del was and what she was capable of. Del had made no attempt to conceal anything.

"And I suppose you came here and cleaned my house just to tell me all about what a shitty person Racheal Graves is and how she can ruin my life. Am I warm?"

"Most people ruin their lives just fine on their own," Del said. "Racheal Graves will end yours."

"Like she could," Davi said.

"There are things worse than dying, kid. Eternity is a long time to live without the people you love," Del said.

Davi's stomach churned. Everyone brought it back around to Alex. "Don't even consider him in this thing," Davi warned.

"I don't, Davida." Del shrugged. "Believe that or not. The truth is what it is. I'm just telling you, watching somebody you love get hurt is bad and livin' the rest of your life without 'em is worse."

Del was speaking truth. Davi knew it. But she also knew

that someday, Del was going to want something and Davi was going to have to make a decision.

"You know what, if you want something from me, let's just get it over with," Davi said. "What do you want?"

Del smiled. "You steer clear of Racheal to start with. I'll be in touch regarding a job." Del got up and walked to the door. "Did you want me to stick around and do the dishes?"

"I want you to go fuck yourself," Davi said.

Del winked at her as she went out the door. "Yes, ma'am."

CHAPTER 16

GAYLE STOOD in front of Davi's desk and handed her the files for the day. There were eleven folders, all different colored labels, and Gayle was popping his mouth open and closed in that fish mouth way. His voice was still monotone, but when he spoke to her, he would stop and twitch, as if the signal got interrupted between his brain and his mouth. Whatever Davi had done when she touched him, she had messed up old Gayle for the long term. Davi took the files and nodded at him. He stood in front of her desk and twitched and blinked.

"Ok, whatever," Davi said as she thumbed through the file folders. She looked up when the little bell above the office door tinkled, and when she saw who walked in, Davi rolled her eyes and sighed. "Great," she said.

Del sat down in the chair across from her and grinned at Davi, then looked up at Gayle. "What the fuck, Gayle?"

Gayle's head twitched as he looked down at Del. He tried to form words, but all he could do was fish mouth at her. Del looked over at Davi.

"What the hell did you do to him?"

Davi didn't bother to deny it. "I don't really know. Anyways, you're the one that messed him up in the first place."

Gayle picked up the pencil cup on Davi's desk and put it back down. He repeated the motion five more times.

"Alrighty, enough of that shit, Gayle. Go on back in your office." Del motioned him away, but Gayle didn't move. He began to stutter nonsense words. Del got up and drug the sputtering Gayle into his office. She shut the door. "You messed him up pretty good, Davida."

"More than you did when you did whatever you did to him?" Davi scoffed.

"Uh, well, yes. When I had him set up he wasn't all cross-wired like that." Del shrugged. "We'll sort him out. Look, I came to take you to lunch."

"I'm not hungry," Davi said.

"Well you can watch me eat then," Del said. "We need to chat."

"You mean you need to bother me and order me to do something I don't want to do," Davi said.

Del smiled. "That's it exactly. Let's go."

"I would, but I don't want to," Davi smiled back.

"I do shit I don't wanna do all the time," Del said. She

stood up and motioned to the door. "I'll make it worth your time."

Davi could see the black trucks cruising the street in front of the office. She didn't have to go with Delilah. There wasn't a physical reason to go because Del couldn't hurt her, but in the back of Davi's mind, she was waiting for that door to open, the door that would let her out of this mess, and she didn't want to miss it when it opened.

Davi sighed and pulled her purse out of her desk drawer. "Make it quick. I need to study for an exam," she said.

Del drove them to a little hole-in-the-wall, old man bar. Davi knew of it but had never had occasion to go in. In high school, kids tried to get in, to get past the old fart that ran it, but he was wise to all the tricks. Davi never bothered. The place smelled of stale cigarette smoke, deep-fryer oil, and Old Spice cologne. Del led them inside to a well-worn round table with comfortable half circle chairs that didn't seem to Davi like they belonged in a bar, more like in somebody's dining room. The bartender came over and placed a tall glass of iced tea down in front of Del. The old woman looked at Davi and croaked, "What do you want?"

Davi recognized another life-time server when she saw one and nodded respectfully. "Water."

The woman nodded back and disappeared.

They heard some yelling, then an old man wandered out of the kitchen. He scowled and wrung his hands as he muttered to himself. When he spotted Del and Davi, he marched over to the table. He looked them up and down and pointed. "You girls ain't old enough to be in here," he said.

"Take it easy Marv," Del said. "We're old enough."

The old man looked confused that Del knew his name. He searched her face, and Davi could see the wheels turning in his brain as he tried to work it out. When he did, his face looked relieved for a second, then it got red and he looked embarrassed. "Why, hello, Delilah. You look different."

"How are you today, Marv?."

"I'm alright, but those damned kids tried to get in here again. I've told them I'll call the law. I'll call their parents." Marv's face contorted, and he looked like he was about to cry. "I think maybe I got confused." He looked at Del and scowled. "I don't think you're old enough to be in here, Delilah."

Del didn't get mad at him. She smiled. "Plenty old enough Marv."

"I'll call Leona and we'll just see. Leona Monroe. Why, she used to work for me." The old man smiled. "She was a tough one."

"The toughest," Del nodded.

The man nodded and started to walk away. "Girl, you ain't old enough and Leona will whip you good when she hears."

"Oh yes sir, I know she would." Del smiled at him.

"You're kind to him," Davi said.

"He's always been a friend to me," Del said. She sipped her tea. "My gran worked for him when I was little. I loved it here." Del nodded toward the ancient jukebox in the corner. "I'd come in here and have lunch and play that old juke. Good memories."

Davi nodded. "Never been in here. Why doesn't the old fella retire?"

"He ain't got nowhere else to go. Family is all dead. Running this place makes him happy."

Davi watched the old man mutter and wipe down the bar aimlessly. "He can't keep this place going by himself." There was nobody else in the place. She doubted if there ever was.

"When that recession hit, he had a tough time. Bank wanted to take it. I took the bank. Marv can putter around here until he dies." Del smiled at the old woman bartender as she placed a cheeseburger and a basket of deep-fried mushrooms down in front of Del. She put the same thing in front of Davi.

"Marv ain't having a good day," Del said to the woman.

"No. Not today, Del," the old woman agreed.

"I'll send Donny over. He'll play checkers with him or something."

The woman nodded. "That'd be good." The woman looked down at Davi. "You need anything else?"

Davi shook her head politely. The old woman nodded at her, then collected Marv, who was crying and trying to dial the bar telephone.

"Annie, this telephone don't work. Did you pay the bill?" he yelled at her.

Davi looked at Del as the woman led the old man away.

She thought she saw a flicker of sadness on Del's face. It was gone in a moment, as soon as Del realized Davi was looking at her.

"Alright Davida. I have another job for you."

The moment of Davi feeling something other than pissed at Del passed, and Davi rolled her eyes. "Of course you do. What is it?"

CHAPTER 17

"IF I DO THIS, we're square," Davi said, sitting in the passenger side of Del's Jeep as Del drove them up and over hills, through hollows and next to muddy creek beds, along back gravel roads that Davi hadn't traveled in years, if ever. She had always lived closer to town, and seldom had occasion to traverse such out-of-the-way country roads. These were township roads—county capillaries—but they were well cared for. While they were gravel, not paved, they had been graded smooth, and the gravel was even and fresh. It was unexpected from a poor township.

"We never was anything but square, Davida. You're the one worried about debts," Del said.

Del turned the Jeep onto a narrow offshoot driveway, again, well-maintained and smooth. Large elms lined the road, making a covered canopy of dark shade, so dark it looked like dusk rather than mid-afternoon. When the Jeep burst through the end of the drive and into the sunlight, the change between dark and light was so abrupt it made Davi blink and shade her eyes with her hand.

They were in a hollow. There was flat place—a creek bottom. The small creek ran along perpendicular to the driveway. A noisy, half-assed constructed plywood bridge allowed vehicles to pass. The flat place was large and wide with many fire rings and circles around it. A few weathered picnic tables and old, beat up lawn chairs were strewn about. A single, burned out tree, black and barren stood in the space, set apart from everything else, like it was ostracized. The flat space ended on two sides—one side a sheer climb up a steep hill, the other a gradual slope up a longer hill that disappeared into the woods. The trees were thick and old, huge gnarled things that grew twisted and untrimmed. Davi realized she was back up in a family hollow, likely Del's family's, and though she hadn't been near it before, it had a certain mythos, whispered about in corners all through the county. You didn't venture out to Nolan Holler. You did, and you likely never made it back in one piece.

Black ruins of houses and trailers littered the place. Davi could feel the history; the hate and misery emanated from every ruined, black thing in the place.

The only new structure was a small metal building, a Quonset hut, half-round and shiny. Del pulled up in front of it and killed the engine.

"What are we doing here?" Davi asked.

"Learning things," Del answered.

Del got out of the vehicle. One of the tall boys—Davi thought his name was Kevin, grim faced and dressed in black —opened her door for her and motioned her out of the Jeep.

"Learning what?" Davi asked as she followed Del to the shed.

Del opened the sliding metal door. Sitting in the middle of the building, tied to a chair, a fat, naked, dirty man cried. He blinked when the light hit him and when he saw Del, he began to plead and sob louder.

"Fucking stop crying, Daryl," Del said.

"Who is he?" Davi asked, a sinking feeling beginning in her gut.

"Well, he used to be one of my guys," Del said. "But Daryl here has lost a lot of money and some other valuable commodities that belong to me of late, so we need to learn from him why that has been happening."

"I-I told you Del… I don't know nothing about it. I didn't get no shipment and I didn't miss—"

"Shut the fuck up Daryl," Del said. She glared at him and he shut up. "So, what I need you to do, Davida, is whammy him with your Truth Fingers and get him to tell me who has been stealing my shit."

Davi had known the request was coming, and she still wasn't prepared to answer. She swallowed hard. She wasn't even sure her power worked that way. She had never really been able to coax any specific truth out of anyone, just the truth they seemed to least want anyone to hear.

"I'm not sure I can do it," Davi said. "Do you have any actual proof? That would be better." Davi almost rolled her eyes at herself for that stupid response.

Del didn't bother acknowledging how dumb it was.

"Just whammy him. I ain't trying to fuck around. He's too dumb to have done any of this on his own. I wanna know who put him up to it."

"Well, if he's too dumb, who's to say he did anything at all?"

Del rolled her eyes at Davi. "Okay, I didn't get to this point in my life by being a dipshit. Now I can make people tell me the truth," Del walked over to Daryl and backhanded him so hard he fell over, chair and all, "But it'll take a while, and time is money. So do your thing and we're off to bigger and better things."

One of Del's goons picked the sobbing Daryl up and set the chair on its feet. Daryl's face was a ruined mess where Del hit him. He snorted blood and snot everywhere as he cried.

"Are you going to kill him?" Davi asked. If he told them what Del wanted to know or even if he really had no idea, Davi was afraid Del would kill somebody else with her standing there. She couldn't be part of that. Not again.

"What do you think I do to dicks who steal from me? You think I call Human Resources and write him up?" Del laughed. "You worried about old Daryl here? Would it make you feel better to know he beats his old lady? That he cheats and steals and buys kiddie porn mags?"

"I don't care what he does," Davi said. "I don't want to kill him. If he's that bad, why do you pay him?"

"Cause up til now, he never missed a payment or fucked up a deal for me. Now I'm missing a significant amount of cash and a whole shipment of goods."

"Maybe it was a fluke?"

Del shook her head. "Nah. Something happened. This fat fuck didn't get jacked like he says he did, 'cause nobody is dumb enough to jack my trucks. He let somebody do it. I wanna know who."

"Promise me you won't kill him once he tells you, if he can tell you. And promise me we're done." Davi stared at Del hard. "Promise and I'll do it."

Del looked at Davi for a moment. Davi wanted to see the wheels turning inside Del's brain, but Del's face was a blank mask.

"Alright Davida. You whammy him and we're even. You can keep your job, and nobody will bother you again."

Davi narrowed her eyes. "Promise you won't kill him."

Del narrowed her eyes right back. She looked over at Daryl and nodded. "Okay."

Davi didn't trust it, but if she were honest, she had to admit that Del had never broken her word. Davi had done the best she could for Daryl. Maybe he deserved it and maybe he didn't, but she wouldn't be part of it.

"I don't know if I can make him tell me what you want to know," Davi said.

"You ain't gonna know unless you try," Del said.

Davi exhaled a long, slow breath. She flexed her hand a few times, almost like she was priming herself, and after the fourth flex, she felt the energy start to flow. Since the first time with Brian, she had at least thought of something when she touched the people. She let it roll through her brain a few times, concentrating hard on the word.

Truth

Davi let it cycle through her mind several times, then focused on it, and let the big waves of crackling energy travel up and down her body. She walked over to Daryl and touched his shoulder. She squeezed it as she repeated the word over and over in her brain.

Truth... Truth... Truth

Daryl screamed and sobbed louder when she touched him. Davi could feel the energy and heat traveling between them, and his shirt burned where her hand sat. Daryl didn't talk. His mouth opened and his face got red.

He's trying so hard not to say anything, Davi thought, so she squeezed his shoulder harder and pumped more energy through him.

Daryl thrashed against the chair and strained at his bonds. He babbled and sputtered as he tried to form words, but he failed. Davi narrowed her eyes and squeezed harder. She didn't stop when his clavicle buckled, and his shoulder squished and cracked in her hand. She couldn't understand why he wasn't telling her the truth. Daryl spit and stammered. He shook and convulsed, then managed to look up at

Davi. She saw the panic and fear in his eyes as his mouth made useless shapes that formed no words.

Davi removed her hand from Daryl's ruined shoulder and stepped back, but Daryl didn't stop moving or crying. He still shook, the energy still moved through him even though Davi had let go of him. He cried as he looked up at Davi.

She watched in impotent horror. She couldn't stop it. She had pumped too much into him. Sweat poured from the man and he began to hiccup. His breath came in desperate gasps and after an interminably long second or two, he exhaled a terrible moan and stopped breathing.

Davi didn't need to check his pulse. She knew he was dead. His wide-open eyes stared at her, and his tongue dripped drool onto the dark dirt floor. The unmistakable smell of shit hit her, and she stood there, unable to move as she realized that she had killed a man.

CHAPTER 18

"DAVIDA?" Del said in a soft, calm voice.

"Don't touch me," Davi said. She stared at Daryl's body. She had been staring at it for a solid hour.

"I ain't gonna, but let's go. Let's get you home."

Davi could feel Del right behind her. She turned slowly and looked at Del. She didn't say anything. Her eyes welled up with tears. Del reached out and pulled Davi in to a hug.

"It's okay," she said.

Davi cried into Del's shoulder for a while. She had no idea what she had done to Daryl to kill him, and she had no idea why he couldn't tell her anything.

"Davi, look, I know it's tough but Daryl—"

Davi pulled back from Del and shoved her. "Are you going to tell me all the bad things you knew about him? That he was a pedophile, a thief, a drug dealer, a pimp?" Davi shook her head. "I don't care."

Del shrugged. "Me neither. I'd have killed that dumbass as quick as I would have looked at him. Wouldn't faze me one bit and not because he was a piece of shit, which he was, but because I just don't fucking care. You ain't that way."

"No, but if you have your way, I will be," Davi spat.

"That ain't true. I wouldn't wish this on anybody like you."

"Then you shouldn't have made me!" Davi screamed. She wanted to punch, to hit, to rip somebody apart. She looked around for something to throw or kick. All there was was Daryl's corpse. Davi balled up her fists and screamed. The noise echoed through the metal building and made the corrugated side walls shake.

Del stood firm, unafraid, but her face was sad.

"Maybe I shouldn't have, but better you know what you can do on a piece of shit like Daryl Barton than on somebody else who don't deserve it."

"So I should fucking thank you?" Davi yelled.

"I didn't say that. I'm sorry you did it."

"Sorry you didn't get your information. Sorry you don't know which one of these other pieces of shit is stealing your fucking money and fucking drugs."

"No. I'm sorry you did it because it's real hard to come back from it," Del said quietly.

Davi knew without touching her that Del was telling her the

truth. That enraged her. She stomped over to the side of the building and punched at the steel until she had a four-foot hole in the wall. She grabbed the jagged edge of the hole and pulled and ripped at the metal, reveling in the awful high-pitched screech the metal made as she tore it. She turned around and stared at Del. She wanted to go over there and throttle Del to death, wanted to watch her eyes pop out of their sockets and her face turn purple as she died. Through it all, Del stood calmly.

"Go on and punch me if you wanna," Del said.

Davi stalked over to her and drew back her fist. She kept her eyes on Del, who stood still, waiting for the blow. But something kept Davi from swinging. She wasn't afraid of Del. She was afraid of herself.

Davi relaxed and exhaled, suddenly drained and tired. "We're done. Take me home."

CHAPTER 19

DAVI SAT in the little diner. Her hands shook as she sipped the hot coffee. Del had taken her home and left her without any other words. Nobody bothered her. Davi didn't go back to Gayle's office right away, but she did need money, so she took a week off then went back. Gayle acted like no time had passed, like she hadn't been absent at all. He handed her ten folders—all the same color—and his stutter was gone. Davi guessed whatever she had done to him had worn off and he was back to normal. That made her feel even worse about Daryl Barton. He would never get back to normal. He would rot.

She hadn't been able to think of anything else. She didn't sleep at all. She barely ate. Alex knew something was wrong, and he stayed quiet and played in his room rather than bug her to play with him as he normally did. She didn't yell at him, wasn't angry or short with him, just silent, and somehow, they both thought that was worse.

What Davi was going to do to get back to some semblance of normality, she didn't know. She couldn't talk to anybody about it. The only person who knew anything was Del, and Davi wasn't going to call her. Davi knew that nobody was going to miss Daryl Barton, and she knew that Del wasn't going to hold that over her, but that wasn't really what was weighing on her mind. How had she done it? Why had she done it? How was she going to keep herself from doing it again? Davi wasn't totally stupid about it. She realized that she had made a conscious effort to pump more energy into the man when he didn't speak. The thing was, she actually cared that he was deifying her. It had been a personal affront to her that Daryl hadn't spilled his guts when she willed it. That anger was what worried her.

Davi was about to finish up and go back to the office, contemplating her sudden turn towards super-villainy, when Rachael Graves slid into the seat across from her.

"You look like you need a friend," Racheal said.

"I need sleep more," Davi replied. "I was just about to go."

"You're having a tough time, Davi. Let me help. I don't want anything from you. Just to help you deal with all this." Rachael reached out and touched Davi's forearm. Davi jerked away like she'd been burned.

"You can't help me." Davi grabbed her bag and went to stand.

"Your mind is going a hundred miles a minute, right?

You've done things you didn't think you could, and you're confused. You're not sure that you can control the magic."

"Magic?"

Racheal smiled and nodded. "Yes. Magic. It's beautiful and terrible all at the same time. Incredibly simple, but it's also incredibly complex. You will have to work at it to control it. But you can."

Davi slumped back against the seat. "What if I can't?"

"You can, Davi. You need guidance. We can help you."

"Who are you and what are you?" Davi asked.

"A Coven. Magic users. My sisters and I. We want to be there for you."

"Witches? Are you serious?" Davi rolled her eyes. She had met some pagan girls in school. The listened to a bunch of Stevie Nicks music and watched *The Craft* over and over. Of course she knew they weren't real witches. Davi also knew witches weren't actually real, but then again, she hadn't thought it possible to be shot twice and live or to kill a man by touching him.

Racheal laughed. "Yeah. Witches. I guess that's a way you could say it. Kind of a stupid, negative connotation for us though."

"I mean, yeah, okay, I get that, but how are you going to help me?"

"Magic is about connection and knowing it's bigger than you. You control it with a clear mind and purpose, and it's important that you realize that you cannot do it alone. We help each other." Racheal motioned between them. "Let us show you. We're having a thing tomorrow night. Dinner. Then we'll work on some exercises. Come meet my group, my sisters. If you get nothing out of it, fine. I'll leave you alone."

Davi wasn't sure. It sounded hokey and she had nobody to watch Alex. "I don't know. I would need a babysitter."

"Bring your son. All of our kids will be there."

"Uh, I don't know." Davi hesitated. A part of her wanted to do it. The other part was scared she was taking Alex to a bunch of looney toons.

Racheal smiled. "We're a family. Seriously, almost everyone has children. Come by about six. It's the address on my card."

"I'll think about it," Davi said as she got up to leave.

"You do that, Davi," Racheal waved at her as she left.

Davi walked back to the office, on the fence about going to the dinner, but Racheal seemed sincere, and Davi knew nobody could hurt her. If they tried to hurt Alex, she would destroy them. The risk seemed minimal and the possible benefits—control, community, peace—seemed many. When she got back to her desk, she dug in her purse until she found Rachael's card. The address was outside of town. Davi knew where it was—a large Victorian house, back from the road and right on the river. It wasn't a dank, burned out hollow in the hills, and Davi wasn't defenseless. Maybe the door was opening after all. She only had to be smart enough to walk through it.

CHAPTER 20

"WHY ARE WE GOING HERE?" Alex whined as Davi pulled into the driveway of Racheal's house.

"It's... for... look, just stop whining. There will be dinner and kids for you to hang out with. It won't be awful," Davi said. She couldn't really answer the question of why they were there except that she felt that she was out of options. She had killed somebody. Unintentionally, but that hardly mattered when somebody died. They were still dead. She had to learn to control the power.

Davi didn't know Racheal, but she didn't know what she was or how to control herself, and that was scarier than a potluck dinner at a witch house.

Witch House? Was that even what you called it? Davi didn't know. She didn't know squat all about witches, and she never really thought she would have occasion to learn, but here she was, walking into a coven meeting with her kid and a plastic container of mustard potato salad from the IGA.

Davi and Alex ascended the steps to the long front porch —a veranda, Davi supposed you called it, too big to be a porch. The floor was pleasantly bleached and whitewashed, and while the whole place looked old—the boards were skinny and the paint patchy in places where old had been scraped and new reapplied—it looked well cared for and loved. Davi had a hand up to knock on the screen door when the inside wood door opened and a little boy with long blond hair blinked at them. The boy's hair was as long as any girl's Davi had ever seen, but she instinctively knew it was a boy from the way he acted—bored and bowed up.

"Who are you?" he asked. He looked at Davi, then at Alex, openly scoffing at Alex's Star Wars t-shirt.

Davi felt a bit of rage boil about the kid, but she tramped it down.

"Is your mom around?" Davi asked. She'd be damned if she'd deal with tiny rude doormen.

The boy looked at her as if he were about to retort some-thing smart. Davi quirked an eyebrow at him and didn't smile. He thought better of it.

"MOM! Somebody's here," he yelled, then left them standing outside the door.

So far Davi was unimpressed. If the kid was that rude, how did that reflect on his parents? She would have taken away every possession Alex had if he ever acted like the blond boy. She was almost ready to turn around and go home when Racheal appeared at the door. She smiled at Davi and Alex, then opened the door for them.

"Hey! Glad you guys made it. Come in, come in," Racheal said as she motioned them inside. The blond boy popped out of a small room with a book in his hand, and Racheal grabbed him by the back of his shirt.

"First, you don't leave guests hanging outside of a door. Doors are dangerous places. You know this." Racheal lightly slapped the boy on his blonde head. "Second, you're rude. Apologize to Davida and Alex."

The boy rubbed the back of his head where Racheal smacked him and scowled. Davi didn't think he seemed inclined to apologize for anything.

"Ow... fine. I'm sorry for my rude behavior," the boy said. He eyed Racheal warily. Her scowl faded, and she smiled at him. "Better. Davi, this is my son Owen. Owen, this is Miss Barker and her son Alex."

"Good to meet you," Alex said. Davi almost laughed when he held out his hand to the other boy, all man-like, as if he were at a job interview.

Owen looked smug, but he took Alex's hand and shook it. "Yeah. Nice to meet you."

Racheal smiled over at Davi and winked. "Davi, is it okay if Owen shows Alex around? I think the kids are playing tag in the backyard."

Davi looked down at Alex. He looked back up at her and nodded. He seemed a bit nervous. His little face was tense and drawn. Davi supposed that was a natural thing. She was proud of Alex for being polite and acting grown up even though the Owen kid seemed like a bit of twat at the first meeting. "Sure. Go ahead." Davi patted Alex's shoulder. "Have fun, bud."

"Let's go," Owen said in a bored huff. He motioned Alex with him back the hallway that led to the kitchen.

Racheal smiled at them. "He's being a real turd lately," she said. "He's twelve going on forty-eight."

"Yeah, all of them get lippy and huffy," Davi said.

"Come on back to the kitchen. Everyone is back here, finishing up dinner prep." Racheal motioned Davi back the same hallway the boys had gone, and Davi couldn't help but feel the same anxiety she had sensed in Alex as she followed.

It wasn't that there was anything weird or bad, just the opposite. The house was clean and carefully curated with books and décor that looked like it belonged in a museum gift shop. It was comfortable, obviously lived in, and it smelled like spices—a pleasant earthy smell, like Racheal.

The big kitchen was open and full of natural light. It was a dream farmhouse kitchen with plenty of counter space and a huge sink. Four other women were cooking, plating food, chatting, and avoiding the pack of children who weaved in and out amongst them, stealing bites of food as they yelled then ran outside. They all smiled at Davi when she entered.

Racheal pointed at each of them. "Diane, Amy, Grace, and Sasha. This is Davi."

Davi felt her face get hot and that shy, intimidated feeling percolate in her gut. "Hello," she said with a slight wave.

Diane cleaned her hands off on a dish towel and held a hand out to Davi. She shook Davi's hand, looked at her for a moment, then pulled her into a hug. "Welcome, Davi. Racheal's told us all about you."

"Really?" Davi said as she tried to exit the hug. She wasn't really a friend hugger, mainly because she didn't have many friends.

Diane smiled and nodded. "She did, and we're so glad you decided to join us."

Amy, Grace, and Sasha also came in for hugs. Davi let them, but was nervously shifting around, uncomfortable with all the contact. Racheal put a hand on the small of Davi's back.

"Easy. You won't hurt us. We're friends," Racheal said low in Davi's ear.

"I'm fine," Davi said, shying away from the touch. It was odd and familiar, and Davi didn't like it. She thrust the bucket of potato salad at Diane. "I brought this," she stuttered.

Diane took it and handed it off to Amy. "We thank you," she said with a small bow.

Racheal looked at the kitchen. "We're eating outside? Yes?"

The other women nodded and went back to finishing dinner. Amy and Sasha began carrying plates of food outdoors.

"Wine, Davi?" Racheal asked.

Davi shook her head. "Ah, no... no thanks. I'm good." She didn't want to drink around strangers, especially not whatever witch wine they concocted.

"Um... okay, you sure?" Racheal asked. "It's not weird homemade witch wine, made of rat spleen and toadstool juice if that worries you." She pulled a bottle out of a small wine refrigerator. "It's actually Apothic, so you know, only the rat spleen." She held up the bottle and wagged an eyebrow at Diane. "Diane's. We're lucky it isn't in a box."

"Oh, like you have such discerning tastes?" Diane huffed. She poked Davi in the arm as she went by. "Racheal pretends to be a wine snob, but she's the first in line at Kroger when Yellow Tail goes on sale."

"I'm not made of money," Racheal shrugged. She smiled at Davi. "Something else? Lemonade? Water?"

"No, I'm good for now." Davi snuck a peek outside. Alex was playing tag with the other kids.

"He'll be fine. Owen is kind of a shit right now, but the others are sweethearts." Racheal stood by Davi and pointed to the kids. There were eight of them, all girls except Owen. They were a diverse bunch. Two of the kids had jet black hair, two were white-blonde, one was black, one Asian, and one Hispanic. They were multi-cultural, and all of the women were white. Davi had never seen any of them before and it was such a small, culturally un-diverse town that Asians, black kids, and a Hispanic kid would be noticed and discussed.

"Are they all yours?" Davi asked.

"Are you insane?" Racheal scoffed. "Owen is mine. Believe me, he's enough."

"Oh, I know," Davi said. "You all live here?"

"Yes. Big grounds. Big house. Sasha is a teacher, so we homeschool. We want our children to have a decent education."

"How do you figure?" Davi asked. "The school isn't good enough?"

"Not even close. They're last in the state in every category," Racheal said. "They're under-funded and the teachers are stretched to the brink. Also, the curriculum is dated and frankly, unenlightened and backward."

"Well, I guess we make do with what we have," Davi said. As a product of the county school system, she couldn't pretend she didn't agree a little with Racheal's assessment, but also, she was local enough to be slightly offended, even if she agreed.

"They're inadequate." Racheal said. "Our kids have tested five grades above where the County says they should be. They get time for music and art, and we don't limit what they can study. They love learning."

"Yeah, well, Alex does too."

Racheal laughed. "I'm sorry. I didn't mean to offend you. Alex is a great kid and he'll be fine, I'm sure. You are. You're furthering your education."

Davi shrugged and nodded. "I guess so." She wondered how Racheal knew that, but in point of fact, she thought she should stop wondering how anyone knew anything about her. Clearly, Del and Racheal had means to any information they wanted.

"Ladies, time to eat," Diane said. She shooed everyone outside and yelled for the children to come. Alex ran up and hugged Davi. His face was pleasantly red and his hair sweaty from the games.

"Hungry, buddy?" Davi asked him.

He nodded but stayed quiet. All the other children piled around the table and started filling plates, their mothers yelled at them, making sure they ate balanced meals. Davi plopped some potato salad and a chicken leg down on Alex's plate. She knew he wouldn't touch any green salads or weirdly spiced food.

"The kids can eat wherever they like," Racheal said, motioning toward the pack of children as they rambled over the lawn and sat at the base of a huge, ancient oak tree.

"You wanna go eat with them, or me?" Davi squeezed Alex's shoulder. He looked hesitant.

"I think them," he said quietly.

"It's okay if you don't want to," Davi whispered in his ear.

He looked up at her. Something wasn't right with him, but she didn't know exactly what. He could be shy around other kids and this was a lot to deal with for him. Davi was the same. In the end he squared his little shoulders and tried to look brave and unconcerned.

"I-I'll go with them," he said, then walked off with his plate toward the tree.

"He's a shy little guy, huh?" Racheal said. They all sat down around the table and began to eat.

"Yeah, he's good once he gets comfortable," Davi said.

"Well, he'll be fine next time, I'm sure," Amy said.

Davi thought that was presumptuous. There might not be a next time.

They ate, the conversation was pleasant, rowdy at times. They all acted like sisters, which Davi supposed they were, poking fun at one another, laughing together. Davi didn't have siblings so she was unfamiliar with the cutting, yet loving banter. After they finished eating, they cleared the table away in about ten minutes and they refused to let her help. Once everything was cleaned up, Racheal nodded at Sasha.

"You take the children in for reading time," she said.

Sasha nodded.

Davi hesitated. She didn't want Alex out of her sight. Racheal knew it.

"He'll be fine, Davi. She's reading them *The Hobbit*. That's all."

Davi stared at her a second and nodded. "Okay."

As Sasha herded the noisy kids inside, Davi stopped Alex and hugged him. "Just chill. I'm right here."

"I know, Mom. I'm not a baby," Alex said. He followed Sasha inside.

"Alright. Davi. Everyone here knows you're special. We can all feel it," Racheal said. She looked around at the rest of the women who all smiled and nodded. "We're not going to make you do anything you don't want to do, but we can help you."

"How? How do you figure you can help me?" Davi asked. She was tired of the line. Nobody had helped her yet. They had just gotten her in progressively worse shit.

"We're going to show you how to control the magic. What you do after that is up to you," Racheal said.

Diane, Amy, and Grace stood at three points in a circle. Racheal stood at the head point. "Davi, stand in the center."

"What? Why?" Davi asked. Her palms were sweaty, and she had a funny feeling in the pit of her stomach.

"It's alright. We're going to call the Corners. It will focus us. You'll be in the middle, and we'll protect you and work to help you control your power."

"Umm... I don't know about any of this," Davi said. "It sounds batshit."

"Everything seems batshit, Davi. You should be dead. You can make people do things, but that isn't it, is it?" Racheal looked directly in Davi's eyes. "It's not just the power of Truth. It's life and death. It's critical you learn to control all of it."

"What are you talking about? I can't—"

Racheal held up a hand. "You can and you know it. You make people tell the truth. Not just any truth, The Truth, themselves unconcealed."

Davi shook her head. "I don't know what you're talking about."

Racheal smiled. "No? Well, righteousness and truth are

sometimes connected with death. The Egyptians believed that. Their goddess Maat weighed the souls of the dead against her feather. She decided who went to heaven and who went to hell. So life and death and truth. Just like you."

"Are you telling me I'm an Egyptian goddess?"

"No," Racheal said, "I'm just pointing out the trinity. You can control all those things. They go together."

"How? How do I control it?"

"We're going to show you," Racheal said. She nodded to the other women.

Davi had no clue what they were doing, but they began a series of incantations in succession. After the other three finished, Racheal began a long-winded call upon some spirit to focus them all and welcome Davi into their circle. Davi felt nothing except awkward. She briefly wished that she had googled witch ceremonies before she had agreed to any of this, but any thought was driven from her brain when she felt the rush of energy.

It caught her off-guard and she reacted physically; she threw her head back and sucked in a huge breath of air, barely stifling a scream. She felt wind whip around her. She convulsed, and all her muscles tensed. When they released and she was able to move and focus, she looked forward and saw Racheal in front of her, smiling. Davi looked down at Racheal, which seemed odd because Racheal was quite a bit taller than Davi. That was when Davi realized that she was hovering about two feet in the air.

She panicked a second, her eyes wild as she looked at Racheal for help.

Racheal laughed and nodded. "It's okay. Just think down. You're in control of it."

Davi did what she said. She tried to calm herself by taking in a few deep breaths, then willed herself down.

It worked. When her feet touched the ground, she tried to glue them to the grass.

"You're fine. Try it again, only this time, think up."

"No fucking thanks," Davi said.

"Easy. You have all kinds of magic energy rolling through you right now. Try and keep a positive state of mind."

Davi decided the time to argue or possibly punch Racheal would come later, after she got rid of the crazy voltage coursing through her body.

"What do I do?" Davi asked.

"Breathe deep, even breaths... okay?" Racheal stepped closer. Davi took in several big, slow breaths, and she felt better. The charge was running through her evenly now. It didn't feel foreign, but rather like a natural part of her, like blood running in veins, if one could really feel that. Davi thought she did now. She felt connected to everything. Every movement, every part of her and the world around her. Davi turned in a slow circle, looking at everything, the trees, the grass. Every shrub and flower glowed yellow-green and throbbed. She saw the life of everything around her. As she turned in the circle, she looked at each woman closely. Amy and Grace both pulsed with light gray energy. It enveloped their whole bodies and the pulsation was erratic. Davi looked closer and swore that she could see their hearts beating in that same irregular pattern, neither able to catch up and beat strong and true. She looked at Diane and saw something else. Diane's energy was dark grey and the beat of it was strong and regular. She narrowed her eyes at Diane. Something about the way the grey waves pulsed around the woman made Davi uneasy, not afraid, but she didn't like it. When she turned to look back to Racheal, she was surprised to see nothing. Davi focused and looked closer and realized it wasn't exactly nothing she saw. Every once in a while, Racheal would barely throb, but Davi could detect no aura, no color at all. Davi had never seen any of this before, but she intuitively knew she was looking at their souls, whatever that really meant. She was looking at their true selves. She couldn't see Racheal's and that bothered her. Davi focused and tried harder, squinting her eyes and gritting her teeth as she let more energy run through her.

Racheal's eyes widened and she stopped smiling. Davi thought she looked like she started concentrating harder too, and that only made Davi more curious and intent on seeing Racheal. Davi began to levitate again, and as she rose, she stared directly at Racheal, who was muttering and red in the face. The other woman sweated profusely as she chanted and held her hands up to Davi.

"Show me," Davi whispered. "*Show me.*"

Racheal's eyes narrowed, and she looked angry for a second. She said something Davi couldn't make out. Davi felt the energy sputter a bit. It surged once through her, then it was gone. She crashed to the ground, out of breath and tingling from head to toe.

"You are much stronger than I thought you were," Racheal said. She held a hand down to Davi to help her up.

Davi didn't take it. She stood up on her own, wobbly and weakened, but she was okay.

"That took everything we had to focus you," Racheal said. Her mouth smiled, but her eyes didn't.

Davi looked at the other women. They were all breathing hard and frazzled, sweaty, and exhausted.

"What did you do to me?" Davi asked. She knew the result; she wasn't sure how they had helped her.

"Gave you a jumpstart," Racheal said. "You're the most powerful conduit I've ever seen, and after a bit of practice, you won't need us to stabilize you."

Was that what they did? Stabilize her? Davi wasn't so sure. She was tired. Their efforts and what she had done had taken a lot out of her, but she also felt energized and full of purpose, something she hadn't felt in her entire life. She hadn't ever felt out of control after that first second of power. She felt alive and focused. Davi thought she could do it again after she rested a bit.

"I think I better go now," Davi said. "It's time Alex was in bed."

Racheal nodded. "You'll come again?" She looked at Davi as if she already knew the answer.

CHAPTER 21

THE NEXT COUPLE of weeks saw Davi spending most of her free time with Racheal and the Coven. They didn't always do the ceremony. Sometimes they sat around and talked about the Universe and magic and everyone's place in it. Sometimes they talked about books and current events. They were all a lot more well-read than Davi. Racheal gave her books to read.

"Seriously, this will blow your mind," Racheal said, handing Davi a copy of *The Second Sex*. Davi took it and read a bit of it, but it was tough. The author seemed to write in circles and Davi felt intimidated. But she didn't feel intimidated when they did magic.

Davi had been exhausted after that first session, but every session after that, she had grown stronger. She was able to turn on the power like it was a light switch now. She was strongest in the Circle, but she didn't need the Circle to access the energy. After a bit of practice, Davi could call up the power whenever she liked. She did it on a whim now, with no fear at all, so long as she was just looking.

That's what she called it—Looking. She called up the energy and she looked at people. Davi was surprised by the rainbow of colors people could appear to be. She wasn't sure why that surprised her—she knew people were different, but she thought of the colors as good or bad, so it seemed like there should be only two, black and white. What she saw was every color imaginable. Some people had light blue, some people navy. Some had orange, a few glowed red, only one person was yellow. She could lose herself in it. It was fascinating. What she couldn't figure out right away was how good or bad a color was. Was black bad? It seemed like it should be bad, but Davi didn't know. Black seemed cliched, like a black hat in a movie signified a bad guy and the white hat signified good, but Davi wasn't naïve enough to believe things could be that simple. She was curious though, and she knew the colors had to mean something, she just didn't know what yet. She was determined to figure it out.

"Why does it have to mean anything?" Racheal had asked her when they were sitting around talking about it. "Is that important to you?"

"Why would there be a color if it doesn't mean something?" Davi countered. "Has to mean something."

Racheal shrugged. "Doesn't have to mean anything, Davi. The world doesn't always work like that, and magic doesn't."

Davi didn't buy it at all. "Nah. It does. I wouldn't be able to do it if there wasn't a reason behind it. I'll figure it out."

"How about concentrate on control and not losing it. It's hard for us to help you now. Every time, the others get a little weaker," Racheal said.

"But you don't," Davi said. The other women were completely spent after a session, and they could only take Davi for about fifteen minutes at a time now. Sasha was the weakest among them, and she had slept for two days the last time they put her in the circle with Davi. Racheal had explained that Sasha was the newest addition and her connection wasn't as strong.

"The Connection to each other keeps us safe," Racheal said. "It's our strength. Sasha will get there. She has to be conditioned."

Davi understood, but once she started down the path, there wasn't any way she was going backward or slowing down. She didn't want to hurt anyone else though, so she practiced on her own after Alex was in bed. She called up the energy and floated around her living room. She progressed to the point where she could do mundane tasks like wash the dishes while levitating. Davi thought that might be slightly irresponsible but so far no harm had come of it, and frankly, it was fun.

She did it at work too, hovering while she made coffee or while she sat at her desk and read. She couldn't levitate objects, just herself. She tried, concentrating hard on making a pencil move across her desk, but it never budged. She asked Racheal, who shook her head and laughed.

"You probably can't affect inanimate objects. Truth and Life. The pencil has neither," she said. "Sorry to destroy your dreams of never getting off your couch again."

"Well I can't seem to move people around either," Davi said.

"Have you tried?" Racheal asked.

"Uh, yeah. Like right now," Davi said. She thought hard about moving Racheal, lifting her up off the ground where they were reclining under the big oak tree, but Racheal didn't move any more than the pencil.

"Don't do that. Don't be reckless," Racheal said. She didn't seem to find it amusing.

"That's reckless? Trying a thing?"

"Very," Racheal said. "There's a cost to everything Davi, and just because you don't appear to be paying it right now doesn't mean it isn't there."

"What's the cost?" Davi asked. That was the sort of thing that worried her. She wasn't a thoughtless person by nature, but the magic was interesting and exciting. She only wanted to see what would happen.

"I don't know, but be careful," Rachael said. "I'm not saying don't practice things or try, just have a care when you do it."

Davi nodded. There was a sense that what she could do was prying. She knew making people tell their truth was

THE HARD TRUTH | 153

invasive and painful for them. Nobody seemed to even know she looked at their aura, or whatever it was, but she supposed that didn't mean that it didn't affect them or that maybe she was seeing something they might not want her to see. It was bad manners to pry and Davi did care about manners.

"What else have you tried?" Racheal asked her.

"Just that and the levitation," Davi said.

Racheal got a funny look on her face. She sat up on the grass and pulled Davi up with her, so they were facing each other. "I want you to try something," she said, her voice quiet and serious.

"Try what?" Davi asked.

Racheal pointed to the little patch of grass between them. She took Davi's hand and ran it over top of the grass. It felt thick and prickly. "Kill it," Racheal said.

"What?" Davi asked. She pulled her hand back away from Racheal like she'd been burned. "No. I can't... I don't want do things like that."

"I think you can," Racheal said. "It's grass. Just try."

"Why? Why would you want me to do that?"

Racheal smiled. "One step at a time. Try."

"I-I don't want to kill anything."

"Okay," Racheal said. "Hang on."

She got up and went in the house. When she returned, she had a pack of matches. Racheal sat back down and lit one of the matches. She dropped it to the grass and blew on it to stoke the flame. The fire wasn't big, but it blacked a tiny circle of grass about the size of a silver dollar before she put it out. She nodded to Davi. "Bring it back," she said.

Davi shook her head. "I can't. Nobody can do that."

"Then it won't be any big deal if you try and fail. So try," Racheal said. "Come on Davi. I know you want to know."

Davi did want to know. She wanted to know desperately, but she was terrified. "What if I can't?"

Rachel shrugged. "Then I guess I buy some grass seed." She held her hand out, palm up. "I'll be right here. I won't let anything happen to you."

Davi put her palm against Racheal's and felt a slight jolt. The energy started to hum through her as she linked their fingers. "I'm not worried about me."

"I'm not worried about either of us," Racheal said. "Go on."

Davi nodded. She squeezed Racheal's fingers then let go. The energy ran through her, head to toe as she sat there. Davi looked down at the burnt spot of grass and concentrated. At first, nothing happened, so Davi willed more energy. It moved through her faster and faster, pulsing and occasionally giving her a little shock. They hurt, but not so much, not enough to make her stop. Davi imagined the grass green and whole again. The shocks were regular now, and they began to be more painful. She held fast and kept her concentration. As she did, she saw it. Tiny green tendrils pushed up from the ground, unfolding and growing fatter and greener as the energy hummed all around her and through her. When the last of the brown patch was green again, Davi stopped. She fell over onto the ground, light-headed and dizzy. The grass was as green and lush as it had been before Racheal burned it.

Racheal clapped and lay down next to Davi. She reached out and tucked a sweaty strand of Davi's hair behind her ear, then cupped her cheek.

"Told you so," she said.

CHAPTER 22

"Why are you still working at that office?" Racheal asked.

"Because I have to do things like pay rent and feed my kid," Davi said.

They sat together on the sofa in the music room, reading, while Grace played piano. Davi had been hoping to work on her powers. She was having a difficult time focusing and seeing people's auras and she wanted to strengthen it. It was important to her and she didn't know exactly why. It was more interesting than making people tell her things, and it wasn't dangerous or intrusive, even if Racheal disagreed. The people had no clue, and it fascinated Davi. Lately she hadn't been able to see everyone clearly and it annoyed her. Even now, she tried looking for Grace's aura and couldn't see much. Davi concentrated harder. She screwed up her face and stared at Grace but the only thing she could see was an occasional wisp of grey.

"Any money taken from Delilah Monroe is blood money," Rachael said. "Quit."

"What about pay rent and feed kid was confusing?" Davi asked.

"Nothing is confusing, Davi, but you need to realize that the end doesn't justify the means."

"Spoken like somebody that has options," Davi said. "I know what that job is but until I find another one, I gotta stay with it."

"You think Delilah is just a drug dealer? Is that what you think?" Racheal put her book down, stood up, and offered a hand to Davi. "Come on. We're going for a ride."

"Where?" Davi asked. "I can't just leave Alex."

Racheal rolled her eyes. "He's with Sasha. We won't be gone long enough for him to miss you."

Davi tried to mount another protest, but it was lame, and Racheal grabbed her hand and led her out to her Range Rover. They drove in to town, then out the other side a ways, to another back hollow. There were five trailers spaced out in it. They were in better shape than some of the trailers in Davi's park. They all had underpinning at least even if the porches were a bit rickety looking. When they pulled up, at least one woman came out of every trailer. In most cases, two or three did. They all studied Racheal's vehicle carefully. To Davi they looked like those African prairie dogs, meerkats or whatever they were called. Alex liked to watch videos of them, and they laughed together as the little creatures all stood up in unison to survey the savannah. Once one came out, they all did.

They seemed to recognize Racheal's vehicle and looked uninterested. They all went back inside their trailers save one woman who limped down her steps and out to the vehicle. The woman had stringy hair and bruises all over her face. A big yellow shiner was fading on her left eye. She had a couple big cold sores.

Racheal rolled down her window and smiled at the woman. "Hello, Lila."

"If Del finds out you was here, we'll all be fucked," Lila said.

Racheal looked at Davi and raised her eyebrows as if to say, told you so. She turned back to the woman. "Lila, tell my friend here what you do out here."

"What do you mean tell her? Everybody knows what we do out here." Lila motioned to all the trailers. "It ain't a secret."

Davi had a pretty good idea what went on. "Yeah, I don't guess I need it spelled out for me," Davi said. "Let's just go."

"This is what Delilah Monroe does. She keeps these women here," Racheal said.

"She don't keep us nowhere," Lila said. "This is just where we are."

"You don't have to stay here, Lila. You can do better. Stop tricking. Stop the drugs. I can help you," Racheal said.

"We don't need your help," Lila said.

"Who beat you up?" Racheal asked.

"None of your business," Lila said. Her eyes darted away, and she touched her face where the bruise was.

"You don't have to be afraid," Racheal said.

"Well, apparently she does," Davi said. "What do you want her to tell you? Just leave her be." Davi looked Lila over. She was awful looking. Scrawny and puffy at the same time. Her skin was blotchy, even where the bruises weren't, and they were all over. She was missing teeth, and the cold sores looked chronic. The woman had a hard life, no doubt, and Davi knew Del had something to do with it, but it wasn't one of the problems in front of Davi at the moment. Maybe she should feel some solidarity with these women—Racheal was obviously trying to lead her to that conclusion, but Davi had been poor her whole life and she knew struggle. Maybe not Hooker Hollow Struggle, but she never found much use in comparisons. Things were tough all over and Delilah Monroe wasn't a hero. Whatever.

Another woman scurried down the steps and whispered something in Lila's ear, then ran back inside. It reminded Davi of a rat. Lila huffed. "If you two want answers, you'll get 'em when Del gets here if you care to wait on her."

In this situation, Davi wasn't afraid of Del, and she didn't care at all if Del knew she came out here, but she doubted a confrontation was in Racheal's plan. That wasn't her style exactly. It was confirmed when Racheal started the Range Rover.

"Lila, I'll never give up on you," Racheal said.

"Fuck you, you uppity cunt," Lila said. She flipped them both off.

Racheal just smiled as she backed out of the drive and drove them back to the house.

"And what was that supposed to show me? That Del does shady business? I already knew that," Davi said.

"I just wanted you to understand that Delilah Monroe's crimes are not victimless. It's not just about selling an eight ball of crystal meth to some toothless tweakers back in the hills. Those women are basically slaves. She maintains them in their servitude. That should make you angry."

"I got enough worries of my own that it don't," Davi said. She got out of the vehicle. Racheal joined her on the passenger side.

"You don't see it," Racheal said.

"See what?"

Racheal shook her head and cupped Davi's cheek. "You think you're different than those girls. You're not. Delilah Monroe is doing the same thing to you that she's doing to them. The only difference is, you're not giving ten-dollar blow jobs."

"You know what? Fuck you." Davi backed away from the touch. She felt the anger swell inside her. She was tired of everyone acting like they knew more than her and that she was just a stupid pawn in everything. Davi knew what Del was. Seeing sad backwoods hookers didn't tell her anything new and Racheal's comparison irked her, mostly because

Davi knew it wasn't entirely untrue. She was stuck and she didn't like being reminded of it.

"You need to hear the truth," Racheal said. "Delilah Monroe took something from me once. I want to stop her from taking something from you too."

"I don't have anything worth taking," Davi said.

"I don't need your powers to know you're lying and that you don't believe that for one second." Racheal pinned Davi against the side of the vehicle. "Quit that job. I'll protect you, and we'll make sure she can't hurt anyone ever again."

For a thousandth of a second, Davi saw something flash across Racheal's face. It wasn't love for Davi or even hatred for Del. It was more like the satisfied look a cat had after it maimed a mouse. Davi saw it, then it was gone, and she wasn't sure if she had imagined it or not. She reached out with the energy and tried to look at Racheal, really look, and yet again, she saw nothing. It was unnerving.

Davi scooted sideways and away from Racheal. "I can't. Not until I find another job," Davi said. She started for the house. "I'm going to grab Alex. We gotta go home," she said.

Racheal grabbed her arm and held it. There was nothing but concern on her face, at least that was all Davi saw. Her gut felt something different, but she couldn't trust it.

"Just be careful. Think. And know that I'm here for you," Racheal said. She pulled Davi into a hug.

Davi gave her a squeeze, then quickly backed away. "I know and I really appreciate it," she said.

Davi collected Alex and shoved him in the car. Racheal

didn't try and stop her. She stood in the drive. Davi saw her in the rearview mirror, watching them drive off. She smiled.

CHAPTER 23

IN SPITE of Racheal's comparison, Davi went to work daily, but she hadn't seen Del since the day with Daryl in the hollow. That suited Davi just fine. True to her word, Del paid her and didn't bother her at all. Davi knew they were watching still, but they had gotten stealthier about it. She didn't see the big black trucks at all.

Gayle was the same. He was basically back to normal—whatever that was for whatever Gayle was—and it left Davi free to study and practice using her powers. She was feeling better about things than she had in a long time. Hanging out at Racheal's was enlightening and she hated to admit it, but fun. For the first time, Davi felt like she was progressing at something—not treading water and avoiding drowning.

Davi was a bit worried about Alex. He was quieter than

normal. She wondered if he had a problem with hanging with the other children at Racheal's as much as they did, but if that was the issue, he wouldn't say. Davi questioned him in a variety of ways, all the normal tactics she used to figure out what was going on with him, but none of them yielded information. She considered making him tell her, but the thought of doing that to her son felt wrong to her and she was afraid to lose control, so she let him be and trusted that if there was a problem, Alex would come to her.

The days passed in a peaceful rhythm of school, work, and friend gatherings. Davi had never had such consistency and stability. The monotony was delightful.

But it couldn't last, and it didn't. Davi knew it was over the second the big sheriff walked through the door to Gayle's office.

He took off his hat and nodded at her. "Miss Barker."

"Sheriff."

"How are you doing today?"

Davi shrugged. "What can I help you with?"

"You seen your ex-husband lately?"

"Well, I can't say that I have an ex-husband," Davi said. "You mean Brian Hill?"

"Yes. His mama filed a missing persons report. Nobody has seen him for a week. When did you see him or talk to him last?"

"I guess I don't know. A month? We don't speak that often," Davi said.

"Why not? You have a son," the sheriff said.

"What do you want me to say about it, Sheriff?" Davi puffed up a little. She let herself look at him, really look, and the big man glowed a pleasant green. She needed to be careful, that thought flashed through her mind, not because his glow told her he was dangerous, but because she was mad and didn't want to say the wrong thing.

"I just asked you a question," he said. "It seems odd a man doesn't talk to you about his son regularly."

Davi laughed out loud. "Does it? Does it really? Come on…"

The big Sheriff shrugged. "Fair enough. You ain't seen him or talked to him lately. That's a fact?"

"That's a fact," Davi said. She hesitated. Maybe Brian was holed up in Charleston with his boyfriend. She doubted Brian's mom or sister knew anything about that. It could help them find him, but she didn't know any more than that, and she doubted the Law had the investigative prowess to do anything with the information. Still, withholding information was as bad as lying as far as they were all concerned. "I don't know details, but he has friends somewhere in Charleston. Maybe he's down that way."

"What kind of friends in Charleston?" he asked.

"I don't know. I told you I don't have details."

"Alright. Well, if you hear from him, you call me." The sheriff put his hat on. He looked around the office with a knowing look on his face. Davi knew the sheriff wasn't fooled by the office front. "Got you a better job now."

"The checks come steady," Davi said.

"That ain't the only thing to worry about, Davida."

"Maybe not, but it's the biggest thing I worry about right now," Davi said.

"We both know that ain't true. Tell Del I said hey." He nodded and smiled as he left.

CHAPTER 24

"I DON'T KNOW what else to tell you, Sherri. I ain't seen him or talked to him." Davi held out her hands to the older woman. Brian's mom tracked her down at the office.

Sherri Hill was a large woman, but they had money, so she always had good hair, expensive make-up, and clothes that came from the department store, not the fat lady section at the Walmart. Today, Sherri's make-up and hair were a mess and she wore ratty yoga pants. Nobody had seen or heard from Brian in five weeks.

"Well, the last time you saw him was when?" Sherri asked.

"A month ago. At the shop." Davi said.

"You know something, Davida. It isn't like him not to call about Alex," Sherri said.

"Give me a break, Sherri. Brian doesn't give a shit about

Alex. I told the sheriff to look for him in Charleston. He told me he had new friends there."

"Horseshit, Davida. I would have known about that," Sherri said.

Oh I seriously doubt you would, Sherri, Davi thought. Sherri was racist and homophobic and pretended to go to Church, so Davi knew quite well how she would feel about her baby boy liking dick.

"If he didn't tell you, that isn't my fault," Davi said.

"He never should have gotten involved with trash like you," Sherri spat. "I told him and told him, but—"

Davi was starting to lose patience. She felt the energy surge in her and when she looked at Sherri, she saw pulsating red and an ugly brown color. "Insulting me ain't gonna find him."

"If you have anything to do with him being gone—"

"And how do you figure I could do that?" Davi asked.

Sherri gave a mean laugh. "Oh I heard all about who you been spending time with." She motioned around the office. "Everybody knows who you're with now. You probably told your criminal girlfriend all about how my boy wrongs you. Who knows what the two of you did to him."

"What? Get out of here Sherri before I call the law."

"Oh call 'em. They know all about you too."

"Get out or I'll throw you out." Davi stood up from her chair, and she let the energy free. She wanted to pick Sherri up and chuck her through the door. It would feel good—to punt the mean old bitch and give her what she deserved. She smiled thinking about it.

Sherri must have seen Davi's face change, or maybe she sensed the energy shift, but she backed away toward the door when Davi got up.

"The truth will come out, Davida." Sherri said as she backed out of the office.

"It always does," Davi agreed. She watched Sherri stomp back to her car and drive away. Davi didn't care for the fact that Sherri made insinuations about her and Del. In her heart, she had known it would be a problem, but she hoped everyone would be scared enough of Del to not say anything.

Everyone was right about Brian. Something was wrong. Although it didn't surprise her that Brian hadn't called her, it did surprise her that he hadn't called his parents. They had plenty of money. Brian liked money but was shit at managing it, so he rarely went long without speaking to his mom. He could have gotten involved with more than he bargained for in Charleston with his boyfriend and whatever crew he was running with there. Davi figured drugs were involved too, and Brain was a dumbass, so things could have easily gone sideways for him.

She knew a way to find out, and she knew she wasn't going to enjoy it, but she figured if she could help find Brian it would at least help Alex. No matter what, Brian was still his dad, even if he was a shitty dad, so Davi picked up her phone and made the last call she wanted to make.

"It's me. I need your help. Can you meet me?"

CHAPTER 25

DAVI HANDED Del the bottle of pop and sat down across from her in one of the kitchen chairs she pulled into the living room. Del reclined negligently on the couch. She took the bottle of pop and smiled.

"Holy shit. You're being civil as fuck. You must really need my help," she said.

Davi rolled her eyes. "Come on, please don't make me regret this."

"Alright. I was just fucking with you. What do you want?"

Davi nodded and sighed. "Okay, what kind of contacts do you have in Charleston?"

"Lots. Why?" Del asked after taking a long drink of the Coke.

"Because I need to find somebody," Davi said.

"Oh, you mean your ex. The one that likes to suck cock?"

"How did you know about that?" Davi asked. Her face felt hot, and she thought maybe Del had been playing with her the whole time. She had known what Davi wanted, and she wanted Davi to have to ask.

"I kept tabs on him right after I met you. He's a dipshit."

"Yes, well, he's missing."

"Yep. And the Sheriff came sniffing around," Del said. She shrugged her shoulder at the look of incredulity that Davi shot her way. "He came in my office Davida. You knew I'd know about that part."

Davi did know. That wasn't a surprise. "How did you know Brian was gay?"

"Well, I do own the gay bar he frequents," Del said.

"So has anyone seen him?"

Del shook her head. "Not to my knowledge, no. Hasn't been down in a few weeks."

"And were you ever gonna share any of this information?" Davi asked.

"I'm sharing it now."

Davi sighed and got up. She walked around the living room. "Do you know anything else? Did he owe money?"

"All over town," Del said. "Liked to snort crank and get banged by big hairy men. Gets expensive to party."

She wasn't sure she wanted to know the answer, but she asked anyway. "Did you hurt him?" Davi asked.

"I did not, Davida. He didn't owe me money."

"Would you hurt him?"

"He ever smack you around? Or hit the kid?"

Davi shook her head. "He never hurt Alex. He never paid enough attention to do that."

"He ever hurt you?" Del asked.

"No. Not really." Davi wasn't lying. Brian was all bluster, but other than grab her arm, he had never hurt her. She had hurt him worse.

"Then I wouldn't hurt him," Del said.

Davi sat down on the couch next to Del and stared at her a second. "Delilah. Do you promise me you didn't do anything to Brian?"

"I promise," Del said. "There's no word about him. And if I don't know, nobody knows."

Davi nodded. "Okay. I believe you. Thank you."

Del finished the Coke and set the bottle down on the old coffee table. "Look, I'll dig. If he fucked up, if somebody did something to him, it'll come out. I ain't you, but I know how to get to the truth of things."

Davi nodded. "I know."

Del's face got serious. Her usual smirk was gone. "You been hanging with Racheal Graves an awful lot."

"None of your business," Davi said, bristling.

"I know you think you know what's up, but you don't Davida."

"Racheal has helped me. I owe her a lot," Davi said. "And it isn't your business who I pass time with."

"She told you I was bad news."

"You are bad news. I didn't need to be told," Davi scoffed. She tilted her head and regarded Del. "She told me you took something from her."

"Yeah, I guess she would see it that way," Del said.

"What was it?" Davi asked.

"Doesn't matter," Del said.

"Well I'd say it matters to her," Davi narrowed her eyes. "Tell me."

"Keep your truth whammy away from me, Davida," Del growled. "I told you, the what ain't important. I coulda taken a stick of gum from Racheal Graves and she would make it into a war."

"I highly doubt that," Davi said. "You had to have done something terrible to her."

"I stopped her from getting something she wanted."

Davi shook her head. Somebody was lying. "That isn't the same thing as taking something from her."

Del shrugged "To her it is. You don't know her as well as you think you do. Don't get in her way. That's my advice."

"The same thing could be said about you," Davi said.

Del nodded. "Yeah, well, fair enough. But she ain't what she claims to be, and if she's helping you, that means there's something in it for her."

"And how are you any different?" Davi asked. "All you want is for me to do shit for you."

"I asked you once."

"And I fucking killed him, Del!" Davi threw the chair against the wall. She hadn't realized it, but she was levitating.

Del stood up slowly and held out her hands. She growled

low. "Easy there Davida," Del said. She gave a little twitch. "Take it down a notch, 'cause I-I..."

Del started to sweat. Like drip sweat. Davi had never seen anything quite like it out of anyone not running a marathon. Del looked scared. Her face was white and her eyes wide as she doubled over in pain. "Stop, this is impossible," she said.

"I'm not... I'm not doing anything to you," Davi said. She felt the energy in the room, but she wasn't directing it at Del on purpose. Davi touched Del's arm and tried to take it away.

Del screamed. She flipped the coffee table out of the way and fell on the ground. "Can't be... can't be happening now." Del threw back her head and began to hyper-ventilate.

Davi could see bones and muscles shifting and moving under her skin. She heard the bones creak and crack. Del panted and screamed louder.

"What is happening?" Davi yelled.

Del's screams were turning into awful, guttural growls. Davi stared in horror as Del's limbs twisted and elongated. Fingers sprouted claws and Del's face rippled, bubbled, and shifted into something that couldn't be called human at all. Del's mouth opened and large canine teeth pushed through her gums. Del looked up at her and her eyes changed color from their normal brown to a yellow, then to black. Del was able to get out one last word before all she could do was snarl.

"Run," Del said.

Del turned away from Davi and ripped off her clothes as her body grew and shifted. Hair sprouted from everywhere and when Del turned back around, she had fully transformed into a hulking monster. The monster snarled and growled at Davi. It crouched and looked ready to spring. Davi backed away slowly toward the door.

"Del... easy... I'm gonna go," Davi said. She felt relief when her hand touched the door knob and she opened the door. The thing that used to be Del snarled and creeped forward. It smiled and bared its teeth.

Davi could see the muscles in its back legs tense, and she knew it was coming for her. The creature growled and jumped. Davi wasn't out the door yet so she threw up her hand instinctively and yelled "STOP!"

The creature was blown back through the air and hit the paneled wall of the trailer. The cheap veneer cracked and buckled, and the trailer shook with the impact. The creature shook itself and came for Davi again, its eyes locked on her. Again, Davi held up her hand, and the thing flew backward. This time, it hit the sink and busted the faucet off. Water sprayed everywhere, and that angered the thing even more. It howled and ripped the sink counter off the wall.

Davi stared at it and watched as it ripped apart her kitchen. It easily popped the door off the refrigerator and threw it across the living room. It was so intent on the utter destruction of the trailer, it lost focus on Davi. She jumped when she felt a cold touch on her arm.

"You have to get out of here now," Jerry said. He pulled back from her, but he kept his eyes on the creature. "She will rip everyone and everything apart."

"What the hell is going on?" Davi asked. She and Jerry backed away.

"I gotta try to keep her in there," he said. He ran over to his place and returned with two jars of white powder. He handed one to Davi. "Ring your trailer in a circle. Go."

Davi grabbed the jar and began to pour the powder out. She got half-way around the trailer and met Jerry. He made sure their lines connected.

"Is that supposed to keep it from getting out?"

"I don't know, but I know she won't like it when she smells it."

"If it just makes her mad, then why the hell would you do it?" Davi yelled. The sound of glass breaking and things crashing against walls came steady from the trailer, as did the guttural growls.

"Well, I don't really have any better ideas. I don't want to get close enough to douse her with it," Jerry said.

"What is it?" Davi sniffed the jar. It smelled like mushrooms to her.

"Wolfsbane powder. It's supposed to make her sick and weaken her. Also can keep them out of places, but I never make it all the way right."

"It won't kill her? Just like, knock her out?" Davi asked.

"Probably," Jerry said.

"Probably? Jerry, you better freaking be sure before I go back in there," Davi yelled. She looked up at the door and saw dents begin to appear. The cheap aluminum of the door crumpled where the thing punched. It would be outside in a few seconds.

"You can't go back in there, she'll—" He stopped and looked at her, realizing that Davi was the one person who could go back in there and not be torn to bits.

"Give me that shit," Davi said. She grabbed the jar from him and squared her shoulders.

"Hit her full in the face if you can. All of it," Jerry said.

The trailer door ripped off the hinges and the creature lurched out on to the porch. The monster threw the door and it landed on the neighbor's old Ford Taurus, smashing the windshield to bits. The monster scanned the area. It was huge, seven feet tall. It stood upright and had bulging, coiled muscles in its arms, which ended in huge hands armed with long black claws. When it saw Jerry and Davi, it raised its head and howled, then it opened its maw and smiled before it growled and coiled to spring. Davi caught it midair and flung it back into the trailer. She didn't bother to open the jar, she smashed it into the thing's face. The white powder coated the thing and it sputtered and spat. Then it began to retch, and black vomit poured from its mouth. It fell over onto the floor and whimpered as it tried to get the stuff out of its mouth and eyes. It cried and whined as it huddled on the floor and vomited. It vomited until it was empty, then it dry heaved until it fell prone on the floor and lay still.

Davi watched as the creature slowly began to shift, the joints and muscles realigned, and the bones cracked and shrank back to normal size. In five minutes, the creature was gone, and Delilah Monroe lay on the floor, bruised, covered in white powder, incoherent, but very much alive.

Jerry came in and stared as Del mumbled and tried to get up but failed. She slipped back down on the wet floor and passed out.

"What the fuck was all that?" Davi asked.

"You sure you wanna know?" Jerry asked.

"No. No I'm really not, but you better tell me anyway," Davi said.

CHAPTER 26

"So, okay... a werewolf," Davi said. She handed Del a glass of water. Davi was mostly surprised that she wasn't surprised by the explanation. She'd sensed something strange about Del, but lycanthropy wasn't one of the possibilities she had entertained.

Del chugged the water. "You got any pickles?" She shivered under the blanket she was wrapped in.

Davi winced as she watched Del shake. The woman was covered in bruises, and Davi could see the muscles spasm and the bones make minor shifts as they popped back in place and healed. Davi couldn't imagine the pain that caused. Del grimaced a few times, but she didn't cry out or complain.

"I don't think so," Davi looked at her trashed refrigerator. Even if she had pickles, the door was gone, and the appliance tipped over and ripped in half. The contents were all over the trailer.

"Got any whiskey?" Del asked.

"Ah, nope," Davi said. "Does it hurt?"

"Really fucking bad," Del said. "Sorry about your place." Del nodded at the destruction.

"Uh, yeah, well... "Davi shrugged.

"I'll take care of it," Del said. She was terse, and Davi detected a contrite, embarrassed tone in her voice, something that seemed unlikely to ever come from Delilah Monroe.

"Oh, yeah. You better," Davi said. She didn't really know what to say.

Del nodded to the door. "There's a duffle bag in my Jeep. Got a change of clothes in it. Can you grab it? It's in the back."

"Um, yeah," Davi said. She was glad for the excuse to leave the trailer. Jerry waited for her outside.

"She'll be okay. She heals quick," he said. He regarded Davi carefully. "How did you make her turn?"

"I have no idea. I got mad and then I sort of lost control." Davi found the bag in Del's vehicle.

"But that shouldn't happen unless it's the full moon. It don't make sense." Jerry furrowed his brow and Davi almost saw the synapses in his brain trying to fire and connect.

"I couldn't control it and I grabbed her. I guess it just happens if I'm not careful," Davi said.

"You're going to want to be really careful around her

then. You can heal from a bullet; you might not be able to if Del rips out your guts. She ain't there, you know, when she's like that. She don't know."

"I figured that out," Davi said.

"Well don't hold it against her, is all," Jerry said.

"I'd say there's plenty to hold against her without that being one of them," Davi said. She looked at his rotting arm. Something about that made her think, but her brain was still trying to deal with what she'd seen from Del and she couldn't put the information together any better than Jerry at the moment. She'd have to let it go for now.

"Be careful, Davi," Jerry said. "You can't lose it with Del, because if *she* loses it, everyone is screwed."

Davi nodded. She left him there in the twilight. His face was still contorted in its thinking look, which would have been funny to her maybe in different circumstances. At the moment, it was just frustrating.

Davi handed Del the duffle bag. Del took it and headed back the hallway to change. Davi watched as Del limped and swayed. She stopped in the middle of the hallway, put a hand on the paneling and steadied herself. She was weak and still healing. Davi got the feeling that she was seeing something very few people had ever seen—Delilah Monroe vulnerable.

When Del came back, she wore a plain black t-shirt and a clean pair of jeans. "Tonight you can stay at a hotel. We'll get you a room for as long as it takes to deal with this mess."

"Not necessary." Davi thought she would call Racheal and go stay there.

Del seemed to sense that and her face was grim.

"It's necessary. I clean up my messes," she said. "I'll have this place dealt with in a couple of days."

"Okay. Whatever."

Del looked around. "Alright. I'll call you when you're all set." She wobbled, and Davi reached out and caught her. Del pushed back off, her face red. "Sorry."

"Yeah, I'm sorry too. I didn't mean to—"

Del held up a hand. "Don't. Just don't. It ain't your... anyway, don't." She took a big breath, steadied herself, and walked out.

Davi looked around at the ruined trailer. It was beyond help. The walls were dented and smashed. The kitchen was completely ripped apart and there was water everywhere. The furniture was shredded. Nothing was in one piece and poly stuffing was strung all over. She had always wanted to leave the place, but she never dreamed this would be the end of her residency, a house destroyed by a werewolf. It would be almost funny to say out loud if it wasn't true. Davi pretty much thought that about everything that happened to her of late. A sense of disbelief and resignation was her permanent state now.

"Well, Alex will be excited about a hotel room, I guess," Davi said aloud. She shrugged and went about the task of packing.

CHAPTER 27

DAVI AND ALEX spent two days in the Holiday Inn Express on the Interstate. Alex was upset until he saw the pool. On the third day, Del called her and told her she could go home. When they pulled into the park, Davi's jaw dropped.

The old trailer was gone. A brand new one stood in its place. Del stood next to her Jeep with her hands in her pockets.

"Did they wash our house, Mom?" Alex asked.

"The old one... wasn't worth it to fix it," Del said.

"What did Jim Ross say about that?" Davi asked. The landlord of the trailer park had something to say about everything.

"He won't say anything," Del said.

Davi nodded. "Well... thanks, I guess."

Del shrugged. "Okay then."

They looked at each other awkwardly. Davi wished Del would just go, but Del stood there.

Their standoff was interrupted by the Sheriff's Bronco that pulled up behind Del's Jeep.

The big man got out of the vehicle and casually approached. Alex got skittish and moved behind Davi. Davi noticed Del bristle a bit, but then she relaxed and slouched against the Jeep.

"Del," the Sheriff said. "What are you doing here?"

"None of your business, Jacob," Del said.

The Sheriff ignored her sullen look and turned to Davi. He looked at Alex. "Miss Barker, I need to talk to you."

"Ok, well... go ahead," Davi said.

He motioned toward Alex. "Someplace else?"

Davi looked down at Alex. She didn't want to send him inside. "Alex, get in the car."

"Why? We're home," he whined.

"Just do it," Davi said. She gave him a little shove toward the Civic. He protested but complied.

"We found Brian Hill," Jacob said.

"Yeah? Well, good, I guess. Where was he?"

"It ain't so good. We found him in a dozen pieces, rotting in the junkyard at the machine shop," Jacob said. He stared at Del.

Davi stared dumbly at them both. Her brain felt slow as she tried to process the words. "You're sure?"

The Sheriff never looked at her. He continued to stare at Del. "Yep. No mistaking him, even in that many pieces."

Davi didn't understand the looks that passed between them. She was having a hard time understanding anything as the blood rushed around in her head and her limbs got tingly. She felt the energy start to move through her, and she saw the colors form up around everyone. The big Sheriff was all dark green while Del's was an ever-changing multitude of colors, ranging from black to almost silver. The predominant one was a sky blue, but it never lingered. It would flash and be gone. Davi began to shake and felt an energy surge.

Davi looked at Del and saw Del's eyes widen as she felt the energy too. "Davida! Calm down," Del growled.

Davi saw the muscles in Del's arms ripple and the panic in Del's face. They didn't want a repeat incident. Davi nodded and calmed, forcing the energy back down.

Davi swallowed and addressed Jacob. "What happened?"

"We don't know. But we'll find out," he said. "We may need to talk with you some more."

"Why? I don't know anything about it. I told you everything I know."

"That's a threat, Davi. He means to scare you, but don't let him," Del said.

"It ain't a threat. It's a fact. Don't go no place. Don't leave town." Jacob looked at Del. "I might need to talk to you too."

"Talk all you want, Sheriff," Del said. She smirked at him. "It'll get you as far as it always has."

"Well, I've learned some since," he said.

"I seriously doubt that," Del laughed.

He disregarded Del and turned to Davi. "You go looking

for trouble and trouble finds you Davida." He walked back to his truck and got in. "I'll be in touch," he said as he pulled out of the driveway.

Davi watched him go and had a sick feeling. She looked over at Del. Davi didn't say anything, but she didn't have to. Del shook her head.

"Wasn't me Davida, but, I guess think what you like." She tossed a set of keys to Davi. "Need anything, let me know."

Davi caught the keys but said nothing as she watched Del climb into her Jeep and drive away.

CHAPTER 28

DAVI DIDN'T GO to Brian's funeral. His mom left a multitude of screaming voicemails accusing Davi of murder and threatening to kill her, so she thought it best to avoid the service. She wasn't sure it was good for Alex to go anyway. He took the news in a strangely wooden way. He wasn't close to Brian, but he was still his dad, so Davi had prepared for what she thought would be the worst when she told Alex, but Alex barely reacted at all. His little face was serious but blank. He nodded and went back to his Legos.

Davi spoke to Racheal about it, and Racheal told her that children react differently than one might expect them to about death as they didn't conceive of it the same way that adults did. Davi wasn't sure about that. Alex understood what dead meant. They went through it when he was five and the goldfish died after two weeks. He had cried and been upset at that, as Davi expected. With his father, he barely looked up from playing.

Davi knew there wasn't a right way for the kid to react, but he had been quiet and distant for a while and had been acting like a washed-out version of himself. He was up and ready for school with no screwing around or complaints. He ate whatever she gave him, no protest, and he picked up after himself. None of that seemed natural or like Alex at all. He was seven. She expected whining and messes and the occasional fit. She also expected giggles and him ending up flopped in her bed and cuddles and stories. Those things were gone, and that had her worried more than his lack of reaction to Brian's death.

"Alex, you ready to go?" Davi yelled back the hallway. They were ready to head on over to Racheal's for dinner. She had backed off for a few weeks because of Del and the new place and dealing with Brian's death, but Davi was making too much progress to stop completely. At this point, she could not only revive small things like plants and flowers, but she could kill them too, although this was not a good feeling for her. The acts took a lot of focus and energy, and they left her tired and weakened. She'd never tried it on anything other than a plant, and she was terrified to take the next step and try it on a creature for fear she wouldn't be able to revive it. Racheal had made some suggestions, but so far Davi had refused them all. It was too big a risk. She killed a man. She didn't want to do that ever again.

Alex appeared at the end of the hallway, a small duffle bag

packed and slung over his shoulder. "I'm ready," he said in a flat tone.

Davi hugged him and kissed the top of his head. "Everything okay, bud?"

"Yes. Everything's ok."

She played with his hair, messing it up. "You sure? You wanna talk about anything?"

Alex carefully smoothed his hair back into the side part. "No. I'm fine. Can we go now?"

That was his permanent state. Not catatonic, but flat. It worried Davi more than anything else.

She didn't press it. She kissed his forehead and nodded. "Yep. Go get in the car. I'm right behind you."

Alex walked away without comment. Davi shook her head. She grabbed her bag and keys from her bedroom. As she exited the trailer and locked the door, she turned and saw the Sheriff and two deputies waiting. One of them had Alex.

"What's this?" Davi asked, a panic growing rapidly in her gut.

"Miss Barker, I need you to come with me," the Sheriff said.

"Why? I have my kid and I have to—" Davi started toward Alex but the sheriff cut her off.

"He'll be taken care of. CPS has been alerted."

"Why? I haven't done anything. I'm not going with you, and you can't take my kid." Davi felt the energy build with her fear and anger. She balled up her fists and tried to control it, willed herself to keep her feet on the ground.

"This can go easy or hard Davida. The easy way keeps everyone else from getting upset," Jacob nodded at Alex. "The hard way? He'll remember that forever."

"The easy way he will too," Davi said. She looked over at Alex. He stared at her and she could see a flash of uncertainty in his eyes, the old way he might have reacted, like a normal seven-year-old. He wasn't looking at the cops though; he was looking at her, like he could see her start to lose control, and from the look in his eyes, Davi knew he was afraid of her. Then it was gone, and he was back to the unemotional, flat state.

She almost cried. Davi closed her eyes and swallowed, squeezed her fists, and tamped the power down. This wasn't the way.

"Call my mom, not CPS. Please?"

Jacob shook his head. "It's done, but I'll call her too. If you come along."

Davi nodded. It wasn't a fight she would win here and the things she would lose were too precious. The way out would present itself. She had to be calm and patient. For everyone's sake.

CHAPTER 29

THE COUNTY JAIL WAS SMALL. When they brought Davi in, they only had one cell, and Davi was not alone. Delilah Monroe sat on the small cot and reclined against the grey concrete block wall in her aloof, unconcerned way. That non-plussed look wiped from her face when she sniffed the air, then whipped her head up to see Davi. Del sat up and turned to Jacob as he opened the cell door and motioned for Davi to enter.

"Fucking really, Jacob? You know she didn't do anything," Del growled.

"I don't know that Delilah," he said. He closed the door and stepped back. "We'll talk to you two in a bit."

"No you won't," Del yelled. She was agitated, face red, and she jumped up from the cot. "It'll go the same as always, Jake. You're gonna look like a fool again."

He ignored her and walked away, leaving them alone.

Davi looked at Del. She had to control her emotions. She wanted to shake Del, make her tell the truth, but she couldn't chance that going the way she thought it might.

Del calmed. Davi saw her suck in a big breath and shake a bit. The muscles in her back and arms rippled. "This will work out. Don't worry."

"How can I not worry? The law hauled me off in front of my kid and called CPS."

Del's face got red again. "I should have known about that," she said. "I'll fix it."

"How could you have known and how do you think you're going to fix any of this?" Davi asked.

"I know everything these idiots do before they ever do it. They're dumb and predictable. And even if they weren't… well…"

Davi understood. Information was Del's real trade. People thought it was the drugs and the prostitution, but those things were a means to the information. The information was where the money was. The issue was if Del wasn't seeing things it meant her sources were compromised, and from her admission of it and the emotion she showed, it wasn't the first instance and it was a problem.

Davi held up her hand. "Okay, whatever. Just… I need a lawyer."

"Don't worry about it." Del plopped back down on the cot. Her demeanor was back to cool and aloof as she stretched out.

"I do worry. I need a lawyer. They have to give me one."

"You don't want the one they'll give you. He's a dipshit. Mine's on it. We'll be out in an hour. Two tops."

"I'm going to need more than just—" Davi sputtered.

Del shook her head. "Nah. You won't. Did they haul you in and ask you questions yet? Did they even ask you anything?"

"No, but—"

"No. They didn't. They don't got shit. This is Jacob trying to shake my tree."

"Shake your tree? What do I have to do with that?" Davi asked.

"He thinks you affect me. He thinks I ripped up your baby daddy because I like you, and he thinks he can catch me using you."

Davi looked at Del for a second or two. "Can he? "she asked.

Del laughed out loud. "Jacob couldn't catch a cold." She sat up and patted a space on the cot next to her. Davi sat down. She was tired, and her brain whirled with these thoughts and worries about Alex.

"I didn't kill him. Even if I did, he'd never catch me. My lawyer will fix it, and she'll get the kid too. I promise. Like it never happened."

"Except it did happen, Del," Davi said. "I'll be in trouble about this with those people. All I ever wanted was to keep Alex safe. Why couldn't you just leave me alone?"

Del stared at her. She wouldn't answer that question and

she looked sad. Davi reached out but didn't touch her. She could make her tell.

"Don't Davida," Del said. "It don't work that way on me, and you know it."

"Then tell me."

"No."

Davi pulled back her hand. "We can't keep doing this. People are getting hurt. Racheal was right about all this."

"That bitch? Look, you think she's one thing but she ain't. I keep telling you—"

"Funny, you keep telling me that, but she isn't the one that got me locked up and my kid taken. She's only ever helped me."

"I didn't do—"

Davi stood up and walked to the other side of the cell. "You did. You have. You ruin shit. That's all you do. She told me, and I guess I should have listened more or done more to... I don't know."

Del shrugged. "Think what you like, but you're missing big problems and when you finally see 'em, I might not be able to stop her."

"I don't need you to stop her. In case you hadn't noticed, I'm not helpless. Nobody can hurt me."

"Now who's lying?" Del said. She reclined back on the bunk and shut down.

Davi sat down on the floor and pulled her knees to her chest. There was nothing more to say.

CHAPTER 30

IT TOOK two and half hours for Del's lawyer to spring them. The woman walked in looking like a stereotypical lady ball-busting lawyer in an expensive suit and severe slicked-back blonde hair. Davi had never seen anyone else like her in town. The woman's heels clacked down the tile.

"They've beaten their previous record for stupidity, Delilah," the woman said. Her voice was loud and grating to Davi's ears. The unfamiliar northeast accent was harsh and brusque to her. The hard r's, staccato, and fast pace of her speech added to Davi's tension.

"Good to have a goal, I reckon," Del said. She stood up and stretched, then approached the bars. The deputy opened the door. Del motioned for Davi to go first.

Davi got up. "What about my son?"

The lawyer maintained eye contact with the sheriff. "Taken care of. He'll be waiting once we get outside," the lawyer said. "I've already filed a lawsuit on your behalf, don't worry."

"No, I don't want that, I just want to be done," Davi said.

When they got to the lobby, Davi was shocked to see Racheal waiting with Alex at her side. Davi went to Alex and hugged him hard. He barely hugged her back.

"Hi mommy," he said.

"Baby. Are you okay?" Davi knelt and looked him over. He was fine physically, but he displayed no emotion at all.

"I'm okay," he said. Alex stared at the wall ahead.

Davi searched his face and tried to control her tears, but they flowed. "I'm sorry, bud." She felt a hand on her shoulder and looked up at Racheal. Davi stood up and hugged her. She buried her face in Racheal's shoulder and held tight.

"It's okay. I got you. He's fine. You're fine," Racheal whispered in her ear.

"He's not. Something's wrong," Davi said.

"Oh something is definitely wrong," Del said.

Davi turned and looked at her. "Leave us alone. We're not your concern."

"Davida, for somebody so obsessed with the truth, you sure are blind to it. Get away from that thing. You don't have to come with me, just get away from her," Del growled.

"Thing? Me? That's ridiculous coming from a monster like you," Racheal said. "Davi is coming with me. Don't contact her. Don't come after her. If you do, you will be dealt with."

"You threaten me? That's unwise, Racheal." Del exhaled slowly and drew herself up to her full height. Davi watched the hatred pour from both women. It pulsed and flowed between them like a dark river.

"That works both ways, Delilah," Racheal said. "I won't let you hurt Davi anymore."

"Davi, don't trust her. You don't wanna come with me, fine, but don't go with her."

"Come on, Davi. Let's go." Racheal took Davi's arm and pulled her toward her.

Davi had enough. She shook off Racheal's grasp, closed her eyes, and let the energy flow through her. She was done caring what anyone else said. She was done worrying about the police. She levitated and focused. All eyes were on her and she yelled. "I don't need you to protect me. Stay away from me or I promise you, it will be the last mistake you ever make."

She screamed louder than she thought she had. Everyone except Alex covered their ears. He stood still, staring blankly. Everyone else looked up at her in awe, and she made the energy jump from hand to hand. Del looked sweaty and sick. Rachael looked triumphant. Everyone else looked scared. The cops all stared at her with their mouths hanging open as the cowered before her. Davi felt a hand touch her arm and looked down to see Racheal smiling at her.

"Let's go home," she said.

Davi slowly descended to the floor. She said nothing to Del, only stared as she collected Alex and followed Racheal out the door.

CHAPTER 31

DAVI AND ALEX didn't go back to the trailer. Racheal coordinated a move and their things showed up at her house. They didn't talk about Davi staying there, it was just the outcome.

Time passed calmly and blissfully. Davi didn't need to worry about babysitters or jobs. She stopped going to school and focused full time on honing her powers. All of her energy and drive went in to doing that now, and Rachael encouraged it.

"It's your purpose and your destiny. Stop fighting it. Stop trying to be something you're not," Racheal said. They were sitting together in the garden that evening recovering after a session.

"And what is that?" Davi asked.

"Ordinary," Racheal said. She reached over and cupped Davi's cheek. "You really think you can get an associate degree in accounting, work some nine-to-five job, get excited about pumpkin-spice season, and that's going to be you? You really think you'll be happy?"

"I have to do something," Davi said. "I can't just stay here and—"

"Yes. Yes you can," Racheal said. "You're doing exactly what you're supposed to be doing here. With me." Racheal reached out and linked their fingers.

Davi blushed at that. Something wasn't quite right. It wasn't what they were doing, how they were living, felt wrong exactly, it just didn't feel quite right. Davi couldn't pinpoint exactly why. Her own truth eluded her.

She stopped thinking about it for the time being and focused on herself and Alex. He was calm and compliant. It was the most upsetting part of the situation. When she tried to draw him out, she got no response. Racheal assured her he was fine and just dealing with the situation and that Davi should just be patient with him.

"Give him time and space to process things. All we can do is stay engaged with him and be there when he needs us," Racheal said.

Nothing further had come of her detainment. She hadn't heard a word from the Sheriff or Del. Whose efforts ensured that, Davi didn't know; if it was Del's slick lawyer or Racheal, fine. There was no evidence to link her to Brian's death, or slick lawyer or not, the police would have come for her. There couldn't have been any evidence to connect Del either or they surely would have heard of her arrest. In any case, with all the other things going on, Davi was glad for the peace.

But as the days turned into weeks and the weeks turned into a month, the peace began to ripple. The stronger her powers got and the better Davi learned to control them, the more she saw. It wasn't just that she knew when people were telling the truth. The colors and weights told her about intent and history. She knew when people were habitual liars and when they were chronically malicious. It was a flood of information and difficult for Davi to manage sometimes. In public, it was a constant stream. At home, it was more peaceful, but things were starting to get more complicated.

Racheal had a lot more activity coming through the compound than just the other women who lived there. She had meetings and calls that Davi didn't participate in, which was okay, Davi supposed, Racheal made a living somehow, and Davi had been occupied with her own issues, but the people that cycled through had dark auras—greys, browns, blacks and they all felt heavy. Racheal warned Davi that it was reckless to spy on people like that, but Davi was learning that the colors meant something. They gave her sense of light or heavy, and when she saw the heavy, she had a strong reaction. At the compound everyone she saw elicited that reaction.

Davi considered discussing it with Racheal, but they had argued about the auras before, and when Davi looked for Racheal's, she still couldn't see it. It worried her, but didn't know what it meant, and Davi had other things to think about, so she tabled it in her mind. Still, Davi knew Racheal was hiding something.

"What do you do?" Davi asked Racheal point-blank one day when they were reading together on the sofa in Racheal's study.

"Like, you mean, for money?" Racheal asked.

"Yeah. What do you do? What do all these people do?"

Racheal looked at her for a moment and hesitated. "Business Investments," Racheal said.

"Ah, no shit. What kind?"

"Why so curious?"

"Why so secretive?" Davi countered.

"Have I refused to answer you?" Rachael asked. She stood up and went behind her desk. It was an authoritarian pose. Davi seemed to remember something about it from a psychology lecture.

"You're answering a question with a question."

Racheal shrugged. "A lot of different investments. You want me to name them all?"

"No, I think you're being evasive and condescending." Davi got up from the sofa and tossed the book down on the coffee table. She went to leave the room. It felt like an untruth and she didn't understand why there was need for it, not unless there was something shady about it.

"Davi, stop being a child," Racheal said. "Sit back down."

Davi looked at her and scoffed. "Are you giving me orders? Sit back down? I'm not an employee."

"I never said that you were." Racheal walked over to her and partially blocked the door.

Davi didn't like that. The orders and the power plays were no better than Delilah Monroe. Davi breathed in but stopped short of flipping the switch. She didn't back down though.

"Don't order me around."

Racheal didn't back down either. "And don't threaten me," she said. "You're special and you are powerful, but you can't steamroll me." She stood there, unafraid of Davi, almost willing Davi to turn on her power and try.

Davi didn't move. She stood her ground and kept her power in check. The air crackled between them a bit, but nothing else happened.

Racheal cocked her head and smiled, then stepped aside to let Davi pass. Davi hesitated, then she concentrated. For a second—a half a second, really—she saw a tiny puff of black come from Racheal. It was only a wisp, but it was the blackest, heaviest thing Davi had ever seen.

It unsettled her deep down, and she felt sick to her stomach. Her disgust must have showed on her face because something changed on Racheal's face as well. It was a smug, knowing look, as if she realized what Davi had seen and worse, she was unrepentant. Racheal didn't care.

Davi wanted to run. She wanted to grab Alex and go, but something in Racheal's face scared her and made her pause. It was a coldness and a cruelty. Davi realized it had always been there, she just hadn't seen it. How could she have been so blind? Had she been so needful to figure out her power that she had ignored what was there all along? Or was Racheal just that good? She had magic powers of her own, Davi knew. But she saw it now. She knew then they could never leave. Racheal wouldn't allow it.

Davi turned and sat back down on the sofa. She picked up her book and pretended to read. Racheal cleared her throat but said nothing. She joined Davi on the sofa. Racheal picked up her own book and put her hand on Davi's thigh, possessively, then went back to what she was doing before the question was asked. Davi stared at the words in the book without reading them. Racheal's hand felt heavy and hot on her leg. Davi wanted to cast it off, to scream, but she didn't. She sat still as she contemplated doors and thought of how, for a second time, she was a captive, waiting for a door to open.

CHAPTER 32

DAVI PULLED the zipper closed on the duffle bag. Her clothes —she didn't have many, just a small bag's worth—that was all she was taking. Alex's bag was packed too. It sat next to hers on the bed. Inaction had always been her weakness. In Davi's life, every time she found herself in a bad way, she could look back to a certain moment of inaction that had made the situation a hundred times harder to navigate. Now Davi aimed to change that.

After the confrontation with Racheal, Davi decided to go. She wasn't a prisoner. That was the old way of Davi thinking. She had power. She had options. She could go to her mom's place. That was always an option. She also knew she could go back to the trailer. Del hadn't contacted her since the day in the jail, but Davi knew with absolute certainty that the trailer was still hers. She had always operated from the

Land of Terrible Choices. She was still living there, and it was time she moved out.

Davi shouldered the bag and grabbed Alex's. As she was about to walk out of the bedroom, Racheal appeared in the doorway.

"What's going on?" she asked.

"I'm leaving," Davi said.

"Why?"

"Do I need a reason?" Davi said. She started for the doorway. Racheal blocked it.

"Yes. You do. What's all this about?"

"I'm tired of being kept. I want my life back," Davi said.

"What do you mean? This is your life." Racheal moved closer. "We're your family."

"Then you'll be okay with me wanting some space," Davi said. She pushed past Racheal and went to Alex's room. He shared it with Owen, who was throwing darts at the wall instead of a dartboard. The chewed-up place in the drywall showed that he was only interested in destruction, not the game. The regular, rhythmic thunks made Davi jump each time she heard them. Alex paid no attention. He sat on his bed, snapping a few Legos together. He wasn't making anything; he simply clicked the plastic bricks in place, then removed them and clicked them in again. "Come on, bud. Let's go."

"Where are we going?" Alex asked. He didn't move from the bed.

"Home. Let's get moving."

"You are home," Owen said. He grinned and looked at his mom. "Right, Mom?"

"We are home," Alex parroted. He didn't look up.

Davi had a horrible sinking feeling. Racheal walked in to the room and sat down on the bed next to Alex. She put her arm around him.

"That's right. You are home." She looked up at Davi. "Put your things back."

"No. We're leaving, and we are leaving now. Alex. Get up and let's go."

Davi reached out to grab Alex but Racheal stopped her. She grabbed Davi's arm instead. Davi wriggled out of the grasp and reversed it. She grabbed Racheal's arm. She flipped the switch and blasted Racheal full on with the energy. When she did, the juice bounced back at her and Davi flew across the room. She crashed into the door jam and the wood cracked. A huge chunk of drywall fell from the ceiling and landed on top of Davi. Owen clapped and laughed as if it were the funniest thing he had ever seen.

Davi looked down at her arm and there was a burned place, black and charred where the energy rebounded into her. Davi watched it heal and grimaced as it did. It wasn't the normal pressure and tingle she felt when she healed. It was pain. She felt every burned, cracked layer of skin knit itself back together. Every cell that renewed and repaired itself seemed to scream in agony and Davi felt every single one of them.

Davi stood up slowly. She glanced down at her arm. The

place was raw and healing slowly, more slowly than normal. No, not normal. She had become accustomed to the extraordinary. Davi healed quickly, but in this, for the first time in a while, she was afraid of a physical thing. The pain made her feel human again. She'd almost forgotten what that felt like.

Racheal got up from the bed and came closer. "Put your things back," Racheal said.

"Alex, come on," Davi said as she backed away from Racheal.

Alex got up and stood next to Racheal. He linked his little hand in hers and stared up at Davi.

"I don't want to go with you," he said. His face was blank and voice flat. It wasn't her son. It was something else.

Davi looked at Racheal. "What did you do to him?"

"I didn't do anything," Racheal said. "Alex isn't going anywhere, and neither are you. Put your things away and come downstairs. We have work to do."

"And if I don't?" Davi asked.

Racheal picked up Alex. He hugged her and laid his head on her shoulder. Racheal rubbed his back as she looked Davi squarely in the eye. "You will."

Racheal put Alex down on his bed and handed him the Legos. He went back to mindlessly snapping them together. She walked over to Davi and cupped her cheek. Davi recoiled. Racheal smiled at her.

CHAPTER 33

IT WOULD HAVE to be in the night, Davi figured. She'd grab Alex and run. But first, she'd have to make it through the day and whatever Racheal wanted. She put the duffle bag back in the bedroom, but she didn't unpack it. It would be ready for tonight.

After a while, she made her way downstairs and into Racheal's study. Diane waited for her. The grey color around her pulsed with weight and drag. Davi had never exactly liked Diane—she had sometimes been condescending and jealous of the time Davi spent with Racheal—but until this moment, she hadn't felt the sense of heaviness and dread that she felt now. She thought maybe it was because she was looking for it. She wanted to see it. Or it could be that all pretense was now gone. Nobody was hiding anymore.

Diane couldn't be bothered to be civil now either. She

folded her arms across her chest and scowled at Davi. "We're headed outside. To the Glade."

The Glade was where they did most of the magic work. It was a covered place set back in a little grove of trees next to the river. Davi loved it out there. It was quiet and peaceful, with a garden and hammocks. It reminded her of a picture she had seen in a Better Homes and Gardens magazine once, a fancy outdoor living space. It was a nice place to pass an evening. She had a feeling she was about to like it much less.

Everyone was there—Racheal, Amy, Grace, and Sasha. Sasha corralled the children, Alex included, over by the fire pit. Davi's heart sank when she saw him there. Whatever they had in mind, Davi didn't want Alex to have any part of it, but there he was, sitting with Sasha, staring into the fire. The other children clustered around him. They sang songs in a language that Davi had never heard and doubted any human could translate. The children stopped and stared at her as she walked by. Their faces weren't blank. They were dark and hateful. Any pretense of little child innocence and joy was gone. Davi stopped, looked at all of them, let the energy flow, and saw black wisps come from them followed by ebbing dark crimson. It was like blood. It welled up and swirled all around them. The little girls hissed at her as if they knew what she was seeing. Davi looked at Owen and he pulsed the same black and crimson. She watched as his colors started to move in a regular pattern. The children's colors mimicked his. Owen pointed and laughed at her.

When he did that the little girls did the same. Alex stared ahead.

Diane pushed Davi forward. Davi turned and looked at her, then pushed the air back with her hand. Diane scooted back ten feet or so and lost her balance, tumbling onto her back. She jumped up and came at Davi, but Davi pushed her back again.

"Enough," Racheal said.

Diane dusted herself off but didn't say anything. She went to stand next to Racheal.

Davi watched her go, then looked at the other women. They were all pulsing grey and brown, and Davi sensed the heaviness in them as well. When she looked at Racheal, all pretense was most definitely gone. Racheal had the most consistent black field around her Davi had seen. It was thick and oily, and oozed all around her. Davi never smelled anything associated with the colors, but if she could, Racheal's would smell like sewage, like the outhouse toilets at a primitive summer camp along about August. The heavy feeling coming from Racheal wasn't just a sense of weight, but of dread. Davi could feel it vibrating all through her.

"Alright. Tonight, we settle up all old accounts," Racheal said. She looked at Diane. "Go get him."

Diane disappeared into the woods, and when she came back a few minutes later, she led Jerry Monroe into the clearing.

Davi hadn't seen Jerry since the night Del turned at the trailer. He looked redder and yet even pastier than he had that last time, but most notably, his arm was missing. The arm Davi touched was gone. A smooth nub at the elbow was all that was left. Jerry wasn't tied up. He appeared to be moving of his own free will, but he didn't look happy. He looked at Davi, then cast his eyes downward and refused to look Davi in the eye.

"What's he doing here?" Davi asked.

"Jerry has been helping us," Racheal said. "Everybody relax. Sit down." She motioned for all of them to sit.

"Helping you do what?" Davi asked. She looked at Jerry. He looked down at the ground again.

"Jerry has been helping us strategically weaken Delilah Monroe for a while now. He helped us get some footholds inside her organization. He provided critical information. He even told us about you," Racheal said.

"Me?" Davi said.

"I would have found out eventually, but yes. He told me about you, and it helped speed things up quite a bit." Racheal bowed to Jerry. "He even convinced Delilah to try to use you to get the information from that poor idiot we charmed."

Davi's stomach dropped and her face got hot. Daryl. They all wanted that to happen. Something else occurred to Davi.

"You killed Brian. It wasn't Del."

Racheal nodded. "No, Delilah did not do that, although make no mistake, she would have. She is a monster, but Jerry is the one who orchestrated that. Who did you use? Those moronic ghouls? It was a perfect gambit. Who would have ever thought a fat, disgusting vampire and two inbred ghouls could be so useful?"

Davi stood above Jerry. A vampire. Davi should have seen that for what it was. She hadn't connected the dots at all. When she touched him and revealed his truth, he rotted because he was dead. He couldn't hide that from her, it was just that she hadn't been open to seeing the truth. She grabbed his chin and raised it, forcing him to look at her. "Why would you do these things? Del is your blood."

"It wasn't supposed to go this way. I just wanted to get Del to slow down. Restore some balance," he motioned toward Racheal, "I didn't think she would hurt anyone else."

"You're as blind as me," Davi said. She looked over at Racheal. "What did Del do to you? She didn't take anything from you. She stopped you."

Racheal smiled. "We're positioned to take control of everything. The only thing standing in the way is Delilah Monroe, and she won't be able to stop me once she's dead."

"So that's it? Your masterplan? You kill her and take over? Get everything you want?"

"It'll be a great start," Racheal smiled.

"Del knows. I don't know how she knows, but she knows it was you and me. You can't kill her," Jerry said. "It's almost impossible, and she'll never let anyone that close. Not even me now."

"It's not impossible," Racheal said. She patted Jerry on the shoulder. "You know a way."

"There's lots of ways, but she won't fall for any of them,"

Jerry said. "Besides, this was never part of the deal. I agreed to help get Del out of the way."

"You think they meant get her to retire to Florida?" Davi asked. "They were always going to kill her, Jerry. Moron."

"No. She said they wouldn't," Jerry said. "Racheal, you promised me."

"Oh, yeah, and people always tell the truth," Davi said.

"How do we kill her, Jerry?" Racheal asked.

"Why are you asking him? Surely anyone as smart and powerful as you must know how. Do it and be done with it." Davi sat back down in the chair.

"I can't get close enough," Racheal said. "Believe me, I'd love to. Watching you do it is going to have to do."

Davi shook her head. "I'm not going to kill anyone."

"You will," Racheal said. She nodded at Sasha, who brought Alex over. Racheal pulled him into her lap. She smiled at Davi.

Davi stood up and grabbed her chair. She flung it off into the woods. "I will kill all of you!"

"Davi, we've been through this, you can't hurt me."

"I can hurt everyone else." Davi looked around at all of them. She could kill them all. It would be easy. She'd do it the right way. Make them suffer. Make them remember everything they did before they died.

"That remains to be seen. You've not mastered that power yet, but I have confidence in you. We'll practice." Racheal hugged Alex close. "He is such a sweet boy."

Davi's heart sank. She couldn't do it with him there. She

didn't want Alex to see that. She didn't want him to see any of it. She calmed herself. Racheal smiled.

"Better. Jerry? How do we do it?"

"I won't tell you." Jerry crossed his arms. He looked terrified but resolute.

"You will." Racheal looked at Davi. "Make him."

Davi walked over to Jerry and smacked him hard across the face. "Tell her," she said.

"Are you kidding me? If we could beat it out of him or torture him, we would have tied him to a pool lounger and let the sun do it." Racheal said.

"I wish I had never known any of this," Davi said. "I was happier before I knew any of this existed."

Racheal laughed. "You're a liar, Davi. You love what you can do. You loved it from the first moment you made Brian tell you his truth. You love the power and the strength. You've never felt any of that before. I know," Racheal said. "I know everything about you, Davida. I know how much you love all of it."

They had talked about it. Davi told her everything, and she really did love it. There were few better feelings than when the power surged through her or when she reached out and looked at the energy field surrounding somebody. That moment when she just knew about a person, there was a power in it, and it made Davi feel strong and alive. It made her feel like she mattered for the first time in her life. It made her feel special.

"Do what it is in your nature to do, Davida," Racheal said.

Davi walked over to Jerry. She flicked on the energy but hesitated. "You know what will happen?" She looked at the nub of his arm. He was dead. That was the truth of him. But it wasn't his only truth.

"I know. I won't hurt Del like that," he said.

"Then why did you do this at all?"

Jerry started to cry. "Del isn't what you think. I wanted the old her back. Before—" He dissolved into tears. "She wasn't always the thing you think she is, and she can't help the other."

Davi focused on him. She saw no color. Nothing came from him at all. When she concentrated a little harder, she felt something, a light sensation. Jerry wasn't bad. He wasn't unkind. He didn't want to hurt anyone. He simply missed his friend, the person Del was before. The problem was, Jerry was stupid.

Davi closed her eyes and sighed. Davi hoped it wouldn't hurt him. "You're sure?"

Jerry sucked in a sob. He steadied himself and nodded. "I'm sure."

She looked at Racheal. "Don't let Alex watch and I'll do it."

Racheal snapped for Sasha to take him. The woman led Alex back to the fire, and he sat down and stared into it. Racheal waved her hands and some kind of wavy force went up between them and the children. They could no longer hear the children or smell the fire. Racheal smiled and held her hands out for Davi to continue.

Davi put her hands on Jerry's fat, pale face. Her touch was gentle, and she smiled at him.

"Will it hurt?" he sobbed.

"Not if I can help it," Davi said.

He nodded. "Don't let them hurt Del."

Davi leaned down and kissed his cheek. "I'll try," she whispered.

Davi cut the energy on and it flowed from her hands and into Jerry. He shook a bit and his eyes filled with tears. His face began to decay. It turned gray and green and the smell of his rot, hot and rancid, hit Davi full in the face. She gagged and almost puked, but she didn't stop or move away. His eyes got wide and he looked up at her like Alex when he was afraid. Davi smiled at him, then pumped all the energy she had directly into him.

Jerry didn't utter a word or cry out at all. He simply turned to dust. In less than a second, he was gone. The dust scattered around the Glade, lost in the light evening breeze. The scent of putrid decay remained.

Racheal stood up and stalked over to Davi. She stopped short of hitting her. Davi stood her ground. "I guess he didn't know," Davi said.

"It doesn't matter," Racheal said. "You're going to bring Delilah Monroe here, and you're going to kill her. If you try any other little tricks," Racheal waved a hand and the sound barrier between them and the children came down. They looked over at Alex. He stood up and walked over to Racheal.

She put an arm around him. "You won't be the only one to pay the price."

Davi looked down at Alex. He wasn't there. His eyes were blank and every so often, he would twitch. She tried to see his colors, but they were gone. Once he had been a beautiful sapphire blue but now there was nothing. Davi cried. She felt hopeless and helpless. There was only one thing she could do.

Davi wiped her eyes and looked at Racheal. "When it's done, I'll be back, and I want Alex back."

Racheal shook her head. "Absolutely not. You think I trust you to kill her alone? No. You'll bring her here." Racheal snapped her fingers at Diane. Diane brought her a big syringe filled with white liquid. "That should knock her out. Do it however you have to do it but bring her here. I want to watch."

Davi took the syringe. She figured it was the same as the white powder Jerry used when Del turned. "She won't be dumb enough to fall for any tricks," Davi said.

"There is one trick she's dumb enough to fall for," Racheal said. "She's definitely dumb enough to fall for it with you. You have an hour." Racheal cuddled Alex close. "We'll be waiting."

CHAPTER 34

THE CIVIC BOUNCED along the gravel road. Davi had never
been to Del's house, so she had no idea what to expect. When
she called Del and asked to meet, she assumed Del would
come to her, but Del suggested Davi come to her house. The
directions she had been given took her way out on a ridge.
There were no other houses, no farms, nothing around for
miles, just green fields and forest. It seemed odd. Little farms
and family homes dotted the county, but they were seldom
more than a few miles apart. Del's place stood alone. It
wasn't a mansion, but it was the nicest house Davi had ever
seen and the most unique place in the county. Modern, with
lots of big windows, it sat on an open place, high on the hill.
It was a beautiful spot, and the view looked out over the
river valley below. The grounds around it were immaculate,
with lush golf course grass and well-maintained, perfect pea

gravel in the drive. Del's Jeep was parked inside the stand-alone garage and the door was open. There were no other vehicles around. Davi pulled her car though the circular drive and parked. Del had told her to follow the path when she got there. It led back around the house to an outdoor living space with comfortable chairs and a huge fire pit. You could sit at the fire pit and see for miles. It was a stunning view. Del was waiting by the fire.

"Hello, Davida." Del kicked a chair at Davi. "Want a drink?" Del held up a tumbler of dark liquid. Whiskey.

"No thanks," Davi said. She sat down in the offered chair. She wasn't sure how to begin.

"I guess she sent you to kill me?" Del asked.

"She's done something to my kid," Davi said.

"Yep. But you can't hurt her." Del took a big swig of the whiskey.

Davi nodded.

"Witches," Del said. "These ones are real cunts." She smiled over at Davi. "I hate to say I told you so, Davida, but I told you so."

"I killed Jerry," Davi said. "I didn't want to but—"

Del sighed and swigged the rest of her whiskey. "He was mixed up with them. I knew it. Didn't want to believe it. I'm getting soft in my old age."

"You were close to him. He wanted to—"

Del held up a hand. "I know what he wanted. It nearly worked. Too bad he was so fucking stupid." She took another long drink of the whiskey. "I figured it out too late, I reckon.

Daryl confused me. He knew something, but her spell made sure he couldn't spit it out. You thought he didn't want to tell you, but that wasn't it. Them witches fucked with his brain. I should have spotted that quicker."

Davi nodded. "Somehow, she can make people forget or repress things. I don't know what it is."

"Cheap parlor tricks. Anybody can do it. She ain't special," Del said. "Fucked us up just the same. Somebody got sloppy because some of my boys they fucked with came out of it with a solid beating. I shouldn't have been able to beat it out of them. Racheal always was lazy, and she recruits dipshits."

"I know you didn't kill Brian," Davi said. "She set that up well."

Del nodded. "That was a good one. Looked like something I woulda done too, except I ain't ever been dumb enough to leave a body to rot where it would be found. I figured it was her when they found him where he worked. Jacob knew I wasn't that careless. I thought I had some time to work on her, but I knew it was too late when I seen her with the kid. Even my lawyer ain't that fast."

"I should have seen it," Davi said.

"I don't know about that," Del said. "She's a powerful witch, and even if she didn't have the magic, she is a real manipulative twat. You saw exactly what she wanted you to see."

"I see her now, though. But I can't do anything about it."

"She wants me out of the way."

Davi nodded. "What is she going to do?"

"Oh probably bring more of those little shit demons into the world. Nasty little fuckers. Maybe bring something worse through. I don't know. Whatever it is, it'll only benefit her and it's likely to hurt a lot of people. I ain't sure she thinks this shit through. She just does it because she wants to be the girl with all the toys. She don't care if the toys destroy everything." Del poured another glass of whiskey from the decanter on the table. "You gonna get on with it then?"

Davi's hands shook. "She wants to watch me do it. She won't trust it if I do it here." Davi pulled a syringe from her pocket. "I was supposed to drug you with that and bring you out there."

"Wolfsbane," Del said. She sucked back her drink in one swallow. "That won't be enough. It's probably shit anyways. Jerry never could get the brew right," Del said. "Doesn't matter. I'll go with you."

"I'm sorry. She's too powerful. She has a protection spell or some kind of power. I can't hurt her," Davi said.

Del stood up and set her glass down. "I understand. It's okay. Let's go."

"I don't want to do this," Davi said.

"Well, I can't say that I want you to do it." Del looked out over the river valley and her face got dark. Davi saw her wipe away a tear. "Or maybe I do want you to do it. I deserve it." Del sucked in a big breath and looked over at Davi. "It'll be okay," Del said. "I promise."

CHAPTER 35

DAVI LED Del back to the Glade. They were waiting.

It had been a silent car ride. Davi didn't know what to say. Del brought the whiskey bottle with her and kept drinking.

When they entered the Glade, Del had adopted a casual, scoffing attitude. Davi knew that was her usual way of dealing with most situations, especially when she didn't want to appear cornered. Del surveyed the area and the expensive chic decorations.

"Nice fucking place. What a bunch of cunts you all are," Del laughed.

"Nice to see you Delilah," Racheal said.

"Okay, look, get on with it. The only thing worse than whatever it is you think you're gonna do to me will be listening to you talk before you fucking do it," Del said. She pulled a chair over and plopped down in it.

"Simple. To the point. I always admired that about you, Delilah," Racheal said.

"Well, the only thing I ever admired about you was your ass," Del said. She looked down at Racheal's backside and scoffed. "That's gone downhill these years, I see."

"It will be a pleasure to watch you die," Racheal said. She looked at Davi. "Do it."

"Alex," Davi said.

Racheal motioned Alex over. He stood next to her and stared ahead, twitching a bit. His mouth made a fish mouth shape. Just like Gayle's

Just like Gayle's, Davi thought. Her heart began to beat wildly when she realized what Racheal had done to him.

"You really are a hateful fucking bitch, Racheal," Del said. She looked at the kid, then at Davi. "You gotta do what you gotta do, Davida. Remember that."

Davi nodded. She stepped close to Del. Davi put her hand on Del's chest and looked up into her eyes. "I'm sorry. I can't hurt her."

Del smiled and leaned down. She whispered close to Davi's ear "You can't. But I can."

Davi's eyes widened as she realized what Del meant. It could work. She looked at Del and pressed her hand harder into her chest. "I'll have to do it fast and I think it's going to hurt a lot."

Del shrugged. "I'm used to it."

Davi nodded. She flipped the switch and pumped all the energy she had directly into Del's chest.

Del threw back her head and screamed.

CHAPTER 36

THE FIRST TIME Davi saw Del turn, it took maybe five minutes in total. That was fast, but it seemed slow to Davi as she watched it, and she imagined it had felt crawling and torturous to Del, whose body had ripped apart during it.

When Davi focused and hit Del with all the energy, the change took only about a minute. Davi watched in horror as all of Del's bones seemed to crack at once, and all her muscles tore and reformed themselves into the hulking beast. When it was done, the monster collapsed on the ground, heaving and whining as it tried to catch its breath and right itself. It tried to rise several times and failed.

Rachel's eyes went wild, and all the other women stood slack jawed as they gaped at Del's new form.

"Do you know what you've done, Davida?" Rachel yelled.

"That thing will kill us all!" She looked over at Diane and Amy. "Kill it. Now."

"How are we supposed to do that?" Diane screamed.

"She's weak. Stab her," Racheal said.

Diane and Amy pulled long knives from their belts, and even though their eyes were wide with fear, they advanced.

Before they could stab Del, Davi dropped to one knee. She held up her palm and shoved them all. They flew backward and landed in a pile. Davi put her hand on Del's hairy, misshapen back. She could feel the muscles desperately trying to heal themselves, and she could hear Del's heartbeat. It beat jagged and irregular. When it faded, Davi's own heart sank. Del's light wasn't just one color. It was an ever-shifting pattern of all the colors, from dark grey to a beautiful light blue. It had been that way in her human form, and it was still that way in the monstrous one, but it was fading now. When Davi reached out again to feel the weight of it, she couldn't settle on one direction—Del was like a see-saw, sometimes heavy, sometimes light, constantly in flux.

Davi smiled and leaned down to the creature's ear. "Not the end for you, not now." Davi closed her eyes and concentrated. She let the energy gently pulse easy and steady from her fingertips and thought of the dead patch of grass. Davi thought of the new blades curling up from the sweet-smelling earth, and envisioned them unfurling and folding out, lush and green as they stretched upward, toward the warmth of the sun.

At first there was nothing. Del's heart had stopped and

she lay still, but Davi kept on until she felt it. The same tingle she felt when she healed the grass. As she concentrated, the shocks came quicker and stronger. Davi smiled and gave Del a solid jolt. Del's heart started again and Davi fell over, breathing heavy as the shocks still moved through her.

Del's eyes snapped open and she snarled. Davi scooted back. Del ignored her, jumped up, and locked on to Diane. Diane screamed as Del grabbed her and ripped her arm off. The woman looked down at the bloody joint and screamed again. Del growled and pulled Diane's head from her body. She threw it across the glade where it hit a support post with a thud that sounded like an over-ripe watermelon.

Amy dropped the knife and turned to run, but Del grabbed her and shoved a clawed hand in her mouth. Del ripped Amy's jaw off, then flung the body aside as Amy bled to death and choked on her own blood.

Grace tried to run too, but Del pounced on her back and bit down into her neck. She shook Grace's body like Davi had seen a dog shake a possum until it died. Grace went limp, and Del threw her down, then ripped her in half.

Rachael had Alex. She stood still with him as she watched everyone die. Del looked up from Grace's intestines and smelled the air. Davi saw her lock on to Racheal and Alex. Del snarled and began to advance on them.

"She'll kill us both, Davida," Racheal said. "Stop her!" Racheal moved Alex in front of her. He stared blankly ahead, seemingly unconcerned with the monster bearing down on them.

Davi reached out and swiped her palm left, focusing all her energy on moving them. Alex flew ten feet to the left and lay still. Racheal didn't move an inch. Racheal looked over at him, then at Davi. Del snarled and flung herself at Racheal. Racheal's scream was abruptly cut off as Del ripped out her throat. Racheal's face was all shock as she reached for the place where her trachea used to be. She gurgled and choked as the creature shoved it's claws into her stomach and twisted. The monster was gleeful about it; she growled contentedly as she shredded Racheal Graves.

Owen stood over Alex and growled at Davi. It wasn't an animalistic growl; it was unlike anything Davi had ever heard. If you dumped hate, rage, deceit, fear—all the terrible emotions in the world into a sound, that was what came from Owen's throat as he looked at Davi. His eyes turned black and the crimson cloud expanded, swirled, and towered over them.

Davi was still weak from healing Del, but she caught her breath and stood up. She wasn't going to let the little demon have him. She steadied herself, focused, and then, Davi let loose. The air crackled around her as she allowed all her energy to course through her. She rose six feet into the air. "Get away from him," she thundered at Owen.

He growled again in response and smiled, then he looked down at Alex and reached for his throat. Davi screamed and flew at him. She crashed into him and pinned him to the ground. Owen spit and growled at her but he couldn't move. The red swirled around them in a hateful dance. Davi placed both hands on either side of Owen's face and she blasted him. He screamed and his child's body contorted and jerked as it changed into a misshapen, lumpy creature. Its dark red skin oozed pus and Davi smelled putrescene and rotten eggs. She blasted him again. The demon screamed, then melted into a rotten crimson mass. The red cloud around him dissipated, and when it did, all the children screamed at once. Blood red clouds erupted from them as well. They all contorted and twitched, then they rotted. Their flesh fell away from their bones in black-green, rancid blobs.

Davi ran to Alex. He was unconscious. She rolled him over and cradled him. She touched him gently on his shoulder and gave him a light tap with the energy. He screamed, then sucked in a huge breath, and screamed again. When he did, Davi saw a black, shimmering cloud come out of his mouth. It hovered over his head, and Davi scowled and reached out with the palm of her hand. "Go away," she screamed. She concentrated all her energy on the black cloud. A terrible screeching scream came from it. When it dissipated, Alex started crying.

Davi held him close. When she looked in his face this time, she saw him. The real him. Fear and confusion were evident in his eyes, but when they found Davi's he recognized her.

"Mommy?" he squeaked in his little voice as he cried.

Davi cried too and pulled him closer. "It's okay baby. You're okay."

"I think I had a bad dream," he said. He clung to her.

Davi kissed his forehead. "Yes. A very bad dream, but you're awake now." She looked and saw his energy field, a beautiful light blue, return to him.

She was so focused on Alex she forgot about Del. She heard the low snarl and looked up.

Del was covered in blood. Bits of all the women clung to her. Her face was a mess of blood and hair, and her clawed hands were caked in gore up to the elbow. She growled louder at Davi and crouched low, circling them.

She would rip Alex apart and Davi couldn't allow that to happen. She put Alex down and stood up.

"Mommy?" Alex cried. He saw the monster and sobbed.

"It's going to be okay, baby," Davi said. She kept her eyes on Del. Del continued to growl and circle them. "She won't hurt us."

Davi held her palms up to Del and spoke in a calm, low voice. "Del, calm down. I know you could control this if you wanted to. Listen to me."

If Del heard her, Davi couldn't tell. The creature growled louder and stopped circling. She crouched down and looked ready to spring.

Davi squared her shoulders and faced Del. "I'll kill you if I have to," Davi said. "I'd rather not though so just—"

Davi screamed when Del sprung at her. She caught her mid-air and held her there. Del struggled and growled louder. She snarled and snapped at Davi, but Davi held her fast. "Del, just... stop," Davi said. She struggled to hold Del.

As strong as Davi was, Del in this form was almost as strong and she was about to break free.

Davi had no choice. She let the energy flow between them. When she did, Del stopped struggling and whined. The whine turned to a loud howl of pain and misery as she began to shift back to human form. Del's arms broke up and out at an odd angle, then popped back in place. Her legs twisted unnaturally as they went from canine anatomy back to human. Del's howls and whines turned to human screams as she changed back. When it was done, she lay prone on the ground, naked, and covered in blood.

Davi went back to Alex and pulled him close as she watched for signs of life from Del. Davi reached out and looked, but Del's color was gone. Davi bowed her head and cried. She put her hand on Del's chest and she let the energy ease out of her and into Del's heart.

It took a few minutes, but Davi heard it—faint at first, but stronger with each beat. In time, Davi saw her color shining brightly. It was a solid blue color, a bit darker than Alex's, but shimmering and beautiful just the same. Davi collapsed in a heap. Alex cried and huddled close. Davi held him as she tried to catch her breath. "It's okay, baby. It's okay."

Del stirred, moaned, and cried out as she tried to use her muscles, which were still knitting themselves back together. Davi scooted closer and put a hand on Del's back. "Easy. Lie still. You might need a minute."

"Are they all?" Del asked.

"They're… yeah," Davi said.

Del collapsed back down on the ground. She put her forehead on her hands and lay still, letting her own brand of magic heal her.

Davi rocked Alex and patted Del on the back at the same time. They all needed to heal.

CHAPTER 37

DAVI PACKED the last of the bags in the Civic and closed the trunk. Alex sat in the back seat, wearing headphones and watching videos on YouTube.

They were parked outside of Del's place. Davi and Alex stayed there two weeks while they healed. Davi saw very little of Del. She spent all of her time with Alex. He was confused. To him, everything had been a bad dream—foggy snippets of information mixed in with dark terrible things. He woke up every night, sweaty and crying from the nightmares. Davi held him close and cried too. She had no clue if the possession would have any lasting effects on him. If she could have brought Racheal back to life so she could die again, Davi would do it. She blamed herself, too. She was his mother. Her job in life was to protect him and she failed.

"Guilt is a useless thing," Del told her one evening. "Best

get over it quick before it fucks up the stuff you got going on right now."

"I should have seen. I shouldn't have taken him out there."

Del had shrugged. "You did the best you could, and you thought you were protecting him. They were cunts for using him. That's on them. Not you."

"How do you do it?" Davi had asked her. "How do you bear it?"

"I drink a lot of whiskey, and sometimes I punch people," Del said. When Davi gave her a raised eyebrow, Del exhaled deeply. "I just do. There's nothing else to do."

Del's aura had gone back to the shifting colors, but Davi noticed it stayed on the true blue more frequently and for longer periods of time. She smiled at Del. "I know."

"You can't stay here, Davida," Del said quietly.

Davi nodded. "Yeah. I'll go live with my mom. I talked to her yesterday. We'll be out of your hair by the weekend," Davi said.

"No. That ain't what I mean," Del shook her head. "I mean you can't stay here. In this town. In this county. In this state, even."

"Ah, well where do you think I can go?" Davi asked. She had very little cash. She had no degree, no job prospects. She wasn't in much better shape than when she started out. Before she knew about vampires and witches and were-wolves and Truth. In fact, she was probably in worse shape.

Del got up from the sofa. She pulled an envelope out of her desk drawer and handed it to Davi. Davi knew what it was before she opened it. Her breath caught. She had never seen that much money in her life.

"There's fifty grand in there. Don't do stupid shit with it and let anyone get suspicious. You're gonna take it and get the fuck out of here."

"I can't," Davi said.

"You can," Del said. She sat back down next to Davi. "First place you go is Columbus. My lawyer. She's got another package for you. She'll set you up. House. Job. School. Whatever you want. You get on a plane. You go have a happy life."

"I can't do that. Del, my mom. School? Alex?"

"Davida, your whole life you wanted to get clear of this shit valley."

Davi nodded. "Yes, but—"

"Me too. It's hard. If it was easy, you wouldn't see so many fat motherfuckers down at the Front Row spending their shitty pay to get blasted out of their minds every night, hoping to take their damn vacation to Myrtle Beach or get the bank to loan them money for a new four-wheeler." Del took one of Davi's hands and held it. "You gotta go. And I can't know where."

"What are you talking about?" Davi asked. "Why can't you know?"

"Because if I know, I'll find you."

They looked at each other for a few seconds. Davi kept waiting for Del to explain, but if she were honest, she didn't need an explanation.

"You're not the monster that you think you are," Davi said.

"I'm worse, Davida."

"You aren't. I can see it. You can't lie to me, although you're really good at lying to yourself." Davi stood up. She stepped closer to Del. "You could come with us. Get out of here too."

Del backed a step away. "It's too late for any of that."

"I thought you said guilt was a waste?" Davi asked.

"Don't mean I don't have plenty of it," Del said. "You're gonna take the kid and you're gonna get out of here."

From her tone, Davi knew it was final. Del got up and left the room. Davi hadn't seen her after that. The house was big and Del always seemed to be away on business. It was only a few days later that Davi was ready to leave. She told her mom they were going, and that she would call her when they got settled. They had a few changes of clothes and some toys for Alex, but other than that, Davi took nothing.

Davi was about to get in the car when Del came out of the house. She walked out to the car and stood by the driver's side door. Davi shut the door and leaned on the car. Del held out a business card.

"My lawyer. She's expecting you."

Davi took the card and put it in her jean pocket. "I don't think this is necessary."

"Davi, you think I'm the hero here, but I'm not. I've hurt people. Lots of people. I've killed more than I can count. I'd have used you sooner or later. Racheal got you first."

"Technically, you did use me first," Davi said.

"Yeah, well… I'll do it again. So, you go. Go do all the things you want to do."

Davi nodded. It might happen like that. Del might use her. Davi knew she might even help willingly. But Davi was starting to trust her instincts about people. She wasn't all the way there yet, confident and sure, but she was pretty close. The problem was, Del wasn't sure, and as Davi watched Del's colors swirl around her—a constantly changing rainbow and a back and forth see-saw of good and bad, heavy and light— she knew that it was going to be a while before Del was sure.

Davi pulled Del into a hug. Del flinched at first, then Davi felt her relax and tighten her arms around her. They stayed like that for a while, then Del let go and backed away. She motioned toward the car.

Davi got in the Civic and shut the door. She started the engine, then she rolled down the window and thought back to the day they met in the IGA parking lot, an almost identical pose. "You know something Delilah, you're right. You aren't the hero in all this, but you don't have to assume the role of the villain. The hard truth is you've chosen it. That doesn't mean you have to keep choosing it."

She didn't let Del respond. Davi rolled up the window, checked Alex in the rearview mirror, and drove away.

ACKNOWLEDGMENTS

I have a hard time believing I write books and people read them. It's always been a dream and I'm grateful to so many people who help me do this thing that I love.

Thanks to the beta readers for this book: Ethan, Ashley, and Charissa. You guys are rock stars. Thank you for taking the time to read through and give me valuable feedback that made this piece better.

Thanks to my critique group: Amber, Diane, Ethan, Roger, and Nikki. Your early feedback shaped this novel and helped keep me going.

Thanks to Jae, who beta read it, is in my critique group, edited it, and did all sorts of other stuff to help me, some of which pertained to writing, but most of it is just her being the best friend you could ever hope to have. This was a tough one, at a tough time, and I annoyed the hell out of her making this book happen, but she kept talking to me. Thank you for challenging me and dealing with my weirdness. You're my favorite writer and my favorite person.

And lastly, thanks to the people who read *Tooth and Nail* and wanted more. I love the world and characters, and I hope you do too.

ABOUT THE AUTHOR

Jessica Raney is the author of six books—two collections of short fiction: *Oddballs* and *Dreadful Pennies*, and three novels, *Tooth and Nail*, *These Violent Delights*, and *The Hard Truth*. She co-wrote a collection of short fiction, *Tales from the Den, Volume I*. Originally from Marietta, Ohio, she now lives in Houston, Texas. When not navigating Houston traffic or writing, she's dealing with her cat/dog/demon/baby, Gimli.

ALSO BY JESSICA RANEY

Also by Jessica Raney

Oddballs: A collection of Short Fiction

Dreadful Pennies: A collection of Short Things

Tooth and Nail

These Violent Delights

The Hard Truth

Co-Authored with Jae Mazer

Tales from the Den, Dark Fiction, Volume I

www.ingramcontent.com/pod-product-compliance
Lightning Source LLC
Chambersburg PA
CBHW071519110726
47908CB00003B/887